BLACK LIGHTNING

Black Lightning

THE STORY OF A LEOPARD

by Denis Clark

ILLUSTRATED BY C. GIFFORD AMBLER

The Viking Press

NEW YORK

TO

CECILY

WHO GAVE SHELTER TO THE WRITER

FIFTH PRINTING SEPTEMBER 1966

FIC 1. LEOPARDS—STORIES
2. CEYLON

PUBLISHED BY THE VIKING PRESS IN MARCH 1954

LITHOGRAPHED IN THE U. S. A. BY AFFILIATED LITHOGRAPHERS

Contents

Foreword

I know that when my husband, Denis Clark, wrote this story of a young leopard, he hoped that it would one day reach many young readers. For the story is a true one, and it was told Denis by an old Buddhist monk in Ceylon, where Denis himself spent his youth, living in that same jungle which he has painted in this book, and learning all that love of the wild which inspired the books he was later to write.

Alas, it was fated that my husband should not return to that Golden Island as he longed to do. Three years ago he died, after an illness brought on by the years of active flying with the Royal Air Force, which won him the Distinguished Flying Cross and a Wing Commander's rank.

I know how much he would have liked to write a foreword telling you how he came to write *Black Lightning*. Though Denis hunted and shot wild animals, as young men always do, he learned when he was young, and never after forgot, that truly there lies a deep (if strange and perhaps unexplained) trust and harmony between mankind and those great kings of the jungle, some of whom also hunt and kill, as men do, but themselves obey in innocence the law of nature.

But hunting cannot make a man a writer and poet of the wild such as Denis was to become. He owed this, he believed, in part to his having learned well while yet so young the beauty and truth of the higher law of harmony and peace in which those kindly jungle folk who were his friends in Ceylon believed. They are followers of "Lord Buddha," he who taught to the people of Asia the law of friendship among all living creatures so many hundreds of years ago, and which many millions there have followed to this day.

So now this beautiful tale once told to my husband many years ago by that old monk in Ceylon comes to life once more, for you, through the magic of Denis's pen. And I feel sure you will like it.

STEPHANIE CLARK

BLACK LIGHTNING

1. The Old Fort

When her time for motherhood came the leopardess chose a strange den. As if long before she had made up her mind on the matter, she led her big dark-coated mate from the jungle to the sea's rim. For a mile they walked down the beach, leaving two lines of twin tracks in the drying sand until, on a little headland, they came to ruins of stone. The male hesitated, tail uneasily swinging, as she entered an opening fringed by shivering, wind-polished grass at the foot of the gray, weathered masonry. Suspiciously he followed her along a narrow, dry tunnel, snuffing the odor of porcupine which hung strong in the musty air. Seeming to know her way, she led him to a small round chamber, an underground storehouse or magazine of the ruined Portuguese fort she had chosen for home.

Here she gave birth to her cubs, a male and a female. The tiny things were born blind, with soft, pink paws and smooth coats which showed little trace of their tribe's distinguishing emblems of countless black rosettes. In the female kitten these existed invisibly, blurred all together, only to show later on as the skin expanded over her enlarging body. But the male cub's coat displayed that difference from all his tribe which was to win him his name. It was darker far than his father's. He was one of those rare freaks of nature, a coal-black leopard.

Although the male leopard had not liked it at the first view, his mate's choice of a home was a good one. The headland was healthy and safe, within easy reach of good hunting grounds. The old fort had been raised on a deserted part of the shore; one of several outposts built long ago by the Portuguese when they ruled the island of Ceylon. Few men ever came here, though often enough a small fleet of outrigger fishing canoes sailed by close in to the sands. Sometimes a few fishermen landed, men with shining brown bodies and bright sarongs kilted high above their knees; but they carried no weapons and were far too busy about their own business to explore the fort or interfere with the leopards.

Inland, the jungle spread unbroken far up and down the coast. At the edge of the sands there were salt scrub and tussocks of gray-green grass. Sand dunes were there, and hollows where the great sambhur stags loved to lie. The sand reared up in big waves as if imitating the sea, then suddenly yielded to forest and spreading parkland with here and there a lagoon. The tunnel by which the leopards had entered the fort stretched on till it came out at last in the bushes among the first sand dunes. Thus, in case of emergency, they had two ways of escape.

For the first few days after her cubs were born the leopardess hardly left them. Only some time at evening or night when she heard the call of her mate did she hurry to join him and feast, returning fast to her young which mewed eagerly for her milk. The kittens grew quickly. Soon they opened wide, innocent eyes. They started to stumble and crawl about in their den, to play little games, spitting and rolling together on the dry, sand-covered floor. Already the male cub was half as large again as his sister. It was he who first staggered unsteadily into the tunnel and would have ambled along it had not his mother hauled him back by the scruff of his soft, furry neck. It was he who first, the leopardess being away, got fairly started down the tunnel's dark, secret road into which only faintest light glimmered from a crack in the floor of the fort.

He was forging along very nicely, his spraddly legs bearing him well, when he saw two big brown eyes. He halted, bracing himself, back curved, hair on end like black bristles. A strong odor filled his young nostrils, powerful yet oddly familiar, for it had hung faint in the lair ever since he had been born. He spat ferocious defiance as the glowing eyes came close and closer still, a snuffly, snorty noise accompanying them. With it there sounded too a curious clicking and scraping, as of dry sticks dragged across stone.

The cub did not give way from his place in the tunnel's center; and whatever it was halted too, snorting but a few inches away. A sharp call came down the passage. The mother leopard had returned by the inland way. Next moment, with a low growl, she had snatched the cub up in her teeth and hustled him back to the den.

As the leopard cub soon came to know, the thing with the

eyes, the snuffle, and the rattle and scraping accompaniment was nothing more dangerous than one of the pair of old porcupines whose home his parents had invaded. The porcupines had been forced out of their original sleeping place, which the leopards now used as their den, but had resignedly taken up new quarters a little way on down the tunnel where in one part it widened considerably. They and the leopards lived amicably side by side.

The male cub was often to meet them as the weeks passed, and he grew ever more and more venturous. He soon learned there was nothing to do if by chance one or other porcupine was met in the narrow passage. A threatening approach only made the beast curl itself into a bristling ball, whose long quills prevented attack. The little cub tried attack once and went squalling back to his mother, who scolded him as she dragged two needle-sharp, black and white daggers out of his sensitive skin. The porcupines' cumbersome bodies would block the tunnel completely. There was no room to pass, no alternative but to retreat; for so long as the cub waited there the porcupine stayed in its ball. If he wanted to go from the den he must leave by the tunnel's far end.

What a world waited for him the first time the cub left that tunnel! The brilliant sun made him blink but its cheerful heat pleased his small body. Half blinded, he focused his eyes, used only to the tunnel's gloom. What had seemed trees became grass which tickled his nose. What had seemed a huge bird was a butterfly, wonderfully colored, at which he struck out with his paw. Slowly and little by little his eyes

took in the long stretch of hot, silver sand, the bushes and trees on its edge, and the gray stone hump of the ruined Portuguese fort between himself and the sea. What was that beyond, that heaving, rolling green mass with patches of white here and there? What made that curious, never-ending sound? He remembered hearing it always, a vague background of noise to the whole of his short-lived life in the fort. But it was much louder now. He would go and explore.

He was halfway down to the sea when his mother caught him and drove him back up the beach. She distrusted that great, restless water. It was something apart from her life, which belonged only to the jungle. She watched over her two cubs as they played in the sand dunes, resolved that they should not go near it. But in the larger cub's heart there lay a firm-set resolution. He must find out what that thing was, that thing which kept tumbling and calling.

His opportunity came within a few days. Mother and cubs lay sprawled in the warm evening sun when she suddenly sat up alert, ears cocked to the jungle. From it there drifted a curious noise, something between the bray of a donkey and the sound of wood being sawn. She knew very well what it was: the call of her mate as he made his way back to a kill. Three reasons prompted his song. One was to tell her he was bound for the feast, to bid her come and join him. Two was to warn away any poaching intruders, human or beast, from the animal he had slain. And three was to give himself courage to drive such intruders away, should any dispute his right. With a bound his mate disappeared into the bushes.

This was the cub's chance. He was large as a spaniel by now, and firm on his legs. He started away down the sands while his sister sat back observing him but did not follow. Like a kitten, he scampered sideways after the small crabs which raced in dozens before him, suddenly popping out of sight down their holes. A shining brown dish-shape lay in his way, and he tapped one paw on its top. It sprang into immediate life, scuttering off down the slope, its four scoop-like flippers hurling sand into his face. He had chanced on a basking sea turtle, scores of which landed each night to lay their eggs on these warm beaches. He sneezed and shook his eyes clear. Here, close at hand, at last was the tempting green tumult. Cautiously he stalked right down to its edge, lifted one paw and dipped its tip into the water.

Men say every seventh wave is a big one. If that be so, then the wave before the young leopard arrived must have been seventh of the last series. He had plenty of time to flick the bright drops from his paw, lick some of them, wondering at their salt taste and the curious play of the breakers. Then one wave, larger than all that had gone before, suddenly hovered above him to break in a deluge of foam, laughing sunshine and spray. The cub was swept off his feet, bowled over, beaten down flat, picked up and dragged out remorselessly by the backwash. He could not swim. He scarcely knew where he was, what had happened to him. Once his head came up, and he wailed piteously to shore. But his voice was drowned by the boisterous song of the sea, and his mother was half a mile off, eating her fill of a deer. Back and forth, ten, fifteen, twenty yards out, the young leopard was washed, borne to and fro by the surf. Then along came another great wave, to fling him back on the warm sands, senseless and limp. As he lay there a native boat rode up through the breakers to beach a score of yards from him.

Out of the catamaran jumped a brown fisherman and his son. They had landed to seek turtle's eggs, which are more delicious than hen's eggs when they are cooked. The young man caught sight of the sodden, small shape on the sand and ran to look at it.

"What is it?" shouted his father.

"A drowned cat. . . . No, it isn't a cat." He lifted it up by its tail.

Water poured out of the little leopard cub's mouth. It dripped out of his eyes and his ears. His black coat was plastered down flat, and his paws hung gawky and helpless. He looked half the size he had been ten minutes before the sea took him in charge. But he was not dead.

"*Aiyo*, my son, look out!" the fisherman suddenly shouted. The young man glanced up the beach. A tawny, black-speckled creature was cantering down it toward him. Quick as thought he sprang into the sea, dropping the cub at high-water mark. He splashed hurriedly through the surf and helped his father push the boat into deep water. When they looked back, all they saw was the long, slinking form of the leopardess hastening back to the fort. The cub's little body was dangling from her strong jaws.

2. The Drinking Pool

As the weeks passed the leopard cubs began to accompany their parents into the jungle. Already they had some training in what they must do for a livelihood. Hares, jungle fowl, squirrels, lizards which hissed and lashed with their tails, were some of the spoil brought home to the cubs by their mother. On these they tried young teeth and claws, stalking and springing upon the limp, draggled bodies, growling and kicking furiously with their hind legs. It was natural for them to crouch flattened out on the ground, eyes intent, utterly still except for the tips of their tails, which jerked restlessly to and fro. Generations of hunters had stored knowledge deep in their brains, the lore of the chase which came as naturally to them as walking or washing their paws.

Although they still used the den for their home the chase took them farther and farther afield as the dry, hot weather laid its fierce hold on the jungle and game moved away to the rivers. The family made a striking and lovely effect as they set off for the day's hunting. First went the male leopard, the father, large and wary and strong. Close behind followed his mate with her lighter coat, lighter build. And after her came the two cubs, half grown now but still fluffy and not disinclined for a game. But already the baby stare had gone from their eyes. Those eyes were alert and tuned for quick vision, immediate action. As eyes, training, and instinct directed, the young leopards pranced through the bushes, or flattened to earth, or leaped silently on their prey. Quiet and quick were they both, but more silent, more swift by far was the larger, male cub. By daylight his raven-black coat was a handicap to concealment in jungle or glade. It was more easily seen than the mottled shapes of his family as they glided almost invisibly among the sunlight and shade. But at evening his color became part of the twilight and shadows, so that as he grew larger and stronger the deer learned to beware of the danger which lurked in the darkness, from which Black Lightning might strike.

It was desperately hot in the jungle now. The trees stood brown and parched with the long weeks of drought. The rivers had dwindled, first to strings of still pools where the boulders shimmered and baked, then to dry, sandy beds where the bears hunting for water scratched holes. The deer and the buffaloes, monkeys and elephants, went in their troops far away to the few mountain-fed larger rivers, which still flowed strongly. Those animals that remained might drink only from small, scattered waterholes, slimy and dangerous. But the leopards did not as yet leave the fort. They knew a rock hole at which they might still quench their thirst, and their hunting was made all the easier by the other animals' need.

This waterhole had been made by men on the slope of a

huge black rock that pushed its nose out of the jungle above the surrounding trees. Long, long ago a hermit had lived on this rock, an old and honored monk of the doctrine of Buddha. When he had spoken his wish the kindly king of his time had had a cave hewn for his dwelling and a cistern cut out of the stone to serve him for drinking and washing. In the rock over the cave the king had had carved an inscription which called such as read it to follow the Buddha's wise teaching: to do harm to no living creature since who knew in what creature's shape they might be born again on this earth? The letters were still to be found there, but so overgrown with rock lichens they could scarcely be seen any more. So the old monk had lived his last days in the jungle, simple and gentle, waiting his time to die and be born once again in this world or a better, as Buddha's disciples believe. He had lived at peace with the wild beasts. The teaching he followed forbade harm to any live creature, and the animals never disturbed him. He had died, and another old hermit had taken his place. He had died too, and another, but after that war had come to Ceylon and the hermit's cave had been forgotten. For many hundred years it had served as a den for bears or wildcats or whatever beasts cared to use it. But the cistern served as a memorial to the old man and his king. From it, a thousand years later, the wild creatures still slaked their thirst.

Each evening now, during the drought, the wild things came to drink in procession. First, about four o'clock, the gay wild pigeons arrived, yellow and lilac-hued birds, and tiny bronze-winged doves with brilliant green bodies. Then came the peafowl, the cock bird with gorgeous-eyed tail, his demure brown hens closely following. The pigeons rose up with a clatter-like clapping of hands as a long red mongoose snaked his way out of the bushes, lapped busily, and then stretched himself, lazily purring in the hot sunshine. Suddenly he jumped up and scampered away.

Out of the trees two brown men stepped silently on their bare, broad feet. Both carried guns, and without hesitation they made for a little rock wall, crescent-shaped and no more than three feet high, which had served as a shelter for hunters for longer than anyone knew. These men were poachers, Malays, come to shoot deer whose meat they would smoke and then sell. In a trice they had ducked down and hidden behind the stone screen.

After that there was a long pause before anything came to the waterhole. A few parrots with long green tails and sharply spying black eyes, flew overhead. They saw the two men and screamed shrilly, swerving away from the rock. Unlike the less fortunate four-footed beasts, it was little trouble for them to fly on for another ten miles to the next pool.

The sky was heavy and still, the air little cooler yet, though the sun was sinking. From the trees not far away there sounded a short, nervous call, repeated again and again. The hunters nudged one another.

"A leopard, my brother," one whispered. "Hear, the monkeys take note of a leopard."

They flattened themselves so that not a trace of them

showed. Only the tips of their guns pointed above the stones.
Without very much cause they were badly frightened of
leopards, but a leopard's skin was worth twenty rupees at
the least. If an easy shot came they would take it.

The black cub followed his parents toward the pool. His
sister romped by his side, but the black cub would not play
with her. His thoughts were intent on the things that went
on in the jungle: the rank smell where wild swine had passed,
a cracked stump into which an iguana had slipped just in
time to escape his quick claws. When his father and mother
halted to glare at the monkeys with their worried faces
and half-frightened, half-hypnotized eyes, Black Lightning
stopped too, and his lips wrinkled back over his sharp, shining teeth. His mother sat down, and the cubs followed her
example, while the elder male leopard disappeared into a
thicket ahead on his way to the rock. He hoped he might
chance on a lonely deer drinking there and did not want his
stalk spoiled by the rest of his family. They were better em-
ployed in distracting the monkeys' attention. Whatever
heard their calls of warning now would not suspect that a
leopard was close to the pool.

It was as great a surprise for the Malays as for the leopard
when he suddenly came out above them on the rock's summit. He saw them first, for of course they had never heard
his approach as he bounded up the steep slope on swift,
noiseless paws. For a moment he stood staring at them. Then
by an unlucky chance one of the hunters turned his head and
looked upward.

This Malay was on his first hunt in the jungle. His nerves were tensed up by his companion's warning that a leopard was near. Ever since that his eyes had swung right and left, uneasy and white and glistening in his round face. Now, suddenly, with a gasp, he swung round and leveled his gun.

His experienced comrade would never have fired at the leopard poised up above them, with nothing between it and them but the steep, bare slope of the rock.

"Do not shoot, brother," he whispered. "Ah, son of fools, what have you done!"

For the other had fired, and as he did so the leopard leaped into the air with a fierce, coughing grunt. For a second it hung silhouetted against the red sunset, hindlegs straddled, front paws clawing as if it were trying to tear the clouds from the sky. Then, to their enormous surprise, the great spotted body collapsed and tumbled headlong down the slope. A few lucky slugs from the hunter's old "gaspipe" gun had hit it fair in the head.

The female leopard heard the sound of that shot. For a few seconds only, she paused, ears cocked and mouth snarling, then she turned and galloped away, her cubs at her heels. Not till they reached the glade nearest to the old fort did the leopardess pause in her flight. Thirsty and wondering, she led the cubs back to the den, but her mate did not return that night or ever again.

3. The Mud Terror

Next day the three left the fort for the last time. It was no good staying there longer. There was nowhere for them to drink now that danger lurked by their rock hole, except for another pool some fifteen miles on. This was too far away from the den, for a journey there and back every day, to be practical. Besides, the hot weather gave them dry shelter within the jungle wherever they needed it.

The lagoon inland of the sand dunes still held water but it was brackish. Here was nothing to drink, yet the leopards paused to gaze longingly at its shining liquid acres and the game that teemed on its surface and about its margin. A few wild buffaloes still stood knee-deep in its shallows, last of the herds which had quitted this part of the country. But the lagoon was gay with a horde of bright-plumaged birds. Pelicans with their pouched beaks and white bodies larger than swans swam placidly in small fleets. Tall cranes, rosy flamingos, black-headed ibises with thin, down-curving bills, all kinds of long-legged, long-necked waders stalked round its edges or circled above its shimmering mirror. Any of them was a tempting bait to the leopards who, besides being thirsty from yesterday, were all three now very hungry.

Reluctantly they left the lovely lagoon and entered the dry, rustling jungle. Through the scorched trees and brown-leaved bushes they padded, where the only green things to be seen were prickly, cactus-like plants. Though their way took them near it, the leopardess would not approach the rock whence that shot had rung out. Caution kept her away, but also her keen senses warned her that something lay there, all that was left of her strong mate now that the hunters had done with him.

She pressed on fast to the southwest, the cubs lagging behind as the hot hours dragged endlessly on. They chanced on no game, for a great fire had lately swept through this part of the forest. All that could flee before it had fled, while the smaller, stumbling creatures, insects and lizards, tortoises and slow, tiny loris, had been trapped and destroyed in the blaze. By midafternoon they had left the black tree stumps behind, but their coats were dusty with ash, their faces soiled with the charcoaled fingers of bushes, and their feet made sore by the stubby, burned daggers of grass. It was then that they came on some monkeys in a tree.

The chief of the monkeys, large as a poodle, with long gray whiskers and hair, leaned forward on his bent arms as a man leans who looks into a pit. "Uk . . . uk!" he called, and the others took up his cry—the warning that all jungle creatures heed, for it tells them a leopard is prowling. The leopardess stared at him hungrily. Suddenly, without warning, she sprang high up into his tree, clawed at its trunk, found a footing, and clambered fast after the monkeys who shook the branches in alarm but whose voices ceased instantly. She climbed with swift ease and precision, her female cub following her, but slower and clumsily. The male cub remained on the ground, sitting close against the tree trunk. Had he been told to stay there?

One, two, three, four, five monkeys exploded out of the branches, hurtling away, flinging themselves out of danger, racing frantically off from one tree's top to the next. But three monkeys still stayed where they were, and one of these was the old leader. They stared at the high-climbing enemy as if fascinated. They sat silent, made no move to go until she was close underneath them. Even then they might have escaped by taking refuge in the topmost, frailest extremities where she could not follow. But they seemed to be robbed of all cunning. Still without sound, with fixed eyes and dazed, furtive movements, they climbed down hand over hand until they dropped one by one to the ground.

What made them leave the safe treetops, their one sanctuary? Who can tell? Perhaps the same fatal witchcraft which makes the rabbit crouch helpless while the weasel runs in to attack. It is all part of the wild's mystery. Nature weaves strange charms into the struggle between those that eat and are eaten; some to aid hunters, some to aid those who must flee. These foolish, half-mesmerized monkeys now started to scamper for shelter.

Spat, spat! The black cub was on them in a flash. Twice his paws struck. The chief monkey and the one nearest slumped head over heels, their necks broken. The third

wretched fugitive careered away to safety while the three
leopards made short work of the crumpled gray bodies. They
left few remnants behind when they went on their way.

That evening they drank at a lake. To reach the water they
had to walk for half a mile over what had been the lake's
bottom of soft, slimy mud. Now that mud was baked hard as
rock, with countless footmarks of animals preserved in it as if
in concrete. At the end of their journey they found a muddy
and shallow pool, perhaps a hundred yards square.

This lake had been made by men about the same time as
the hermit's cave had been cut. Its purpose, and that of a
hundred more lakes, great and small, dotted over the island,
was to hold water through the dry season so that rice might
be grown the year round. But now, after three months of
burning drought, the lake was all but dried up.

The leopardess and her two cubs marched over this desolate mud-waste as the sky grew red toward night. A small
village stood far away on the lake's other side, little thatched
houses shaded by mango and breadfruit trees, with groves of
coconut palms. Gray smoke from its cooking fires hung low
over the roofs, and through the still air they heard the cries
of the field watchers, the men who spent all night in huts
to keep the wild beasts from their crops. They heard a dog
barking too, *yap-yap-yap*, never ceasing, his only answer a
long-drawn wail from a jackal. The leopardess halted, her
black shadow stretching before her. She cocked her ears to
that yapping, for dogs are a prime dish for leopards and
she was hungry still.

The water was dirty and brown, though it shone blood-red in the sunset. Here and there on its margin lay scattered bones and horns. But they lapped it up greedily, the cubs as a matter of course following their mother's lead to the drinking place she had selected. When they had finished they sat there for a while longer, cleansing their fur while the mother stared longingly at a big, lone buffalo bull which was coming to water. It was too strong a monster for her to think of attacking, but to her famished eyes it appeared as a huge feast parading past on its four mud-splashed legs, an array of choice steaks, finest sirloins, brisket, and chops.

The black cub finished his washing. He looked at the red-hued water, noting what seemed a rough raft of long, knotted logs afloat on its surface. Half a dozen round objects bobbed about close to the shore. He strolled down to see what they were.

He did not hear his mother's low, warning growl. He was far too interested in those curious, bobbing things, each of which he now saw bore two eyes that goggled vacantly at him. He approached as close as he could, even into the soft, liquid mud on the edge of the water, where he was rewarded by seeing one round object emerge on the end of a snaky neck. Its owner, a big black mud-turtle, climbed awkwardly on to a rock and spraddled itself on the top.

And then a dreadful thing happened. With a hideous flurry and squelch some enormous thing rose from the mud and rushed at the cub. It swung round and *swish!* Its long, powerful tail lashed across where he had been standing. But the

black cub stood there no longer. In spite of his careless ignorance some extra sense warned him in time. His leap carried
him over the crocodile's treacherous tail, missing it only by
inches. He ran to his mother and sister while the reptile,
thwarted and angry dashed back into the mud whence it
came. Then the leopard cub's young eyes were opened. What
he had thought was a raft, what had seemed logs idly float-
ing or partly submerged on the bank, he now saw were
scores, hundreds of crocodiles. Disturbed by the rush of
their comrade they shifted and slithered, jostled and
scrambled together, nudged and sludged in the mud. The
water was thick with their horrible, white-bellied bodies,
their gaping mouths and evil, horny-bumped eyes. As the
rivers and pools of the jungle dried up for miles on each side,
the crocodiles had journeyed here to this last patch of shelter-
ing water. They had come till there seemed barely room to
contain them as the pool shrank day after day.

4. The Night Walkers

Though the cubs were weary and would have slept all through the night the leopardess did not rest long. When the full moon rose over the trees she grew restless and called them to follow. They started again down a straight, broad track which ran roughly in the direction she wanted to take.

All the time now her mind was fixed on the need for something to eat. Those monkeys had been a mere snack. Wild leopards are active beasts and they need a great deal of meat to support their energy. Every now and again she would pause to listen for some creature that moved in the trees by the path's side. When she halted the cubs halted too, their ears cocked, the three pairs of eyes glowing red, piercing the shadows. The leopardess opened her jaws to sing her tribe's hunting chant, which is made by sucking in air on one side of the mouth and driving it out on the other. "*See-saw, see-saw!*" she sang, and the young ones took up the cry in their cracked, half-kittenish voices. Then all three would stop suddenly, listening to hear if anything near moved or called, disturbed by their song.

The moonlight flooded their road, but the trees made a tall black wall which screened many mysteries. Something grumbled and rumbled, snapping down branches and twigs, but the leopardess paid no attention. She knew what it was well enough: an old elephant on its own, surly with loneliness. Without leaving the track they passed by an ancient temple, its tall tapering roofs covered over with figures of beasts, men, and gods, all lit by the moon. Bells jingled there, and a horn sounded. This Hindu temple stood by itself in the forest, far away from a road. Only its priests stayed there now, but once a year the roads to it were crowded with pilgrims who came to worship its gods.

Two miles farther on the leopardess suddenly crouched. Something black crackled out of the bushes on to the track and scampered across. Like three dark streaks the leopards dashed after it, tearing into the trees, their eyes like lamps in the darkness. The leopardess caught a strong smell of wild pig in her nostrils. A shadow darted before her, its horny feet thudding over the iron hard ground. She flung herself through the air. The pig squealed as her claws struck its neck and it felt her weight riding its body. Next moment they tumbled together, grunting and struggling. The cubs had not lagged far behind her, and soon all three had feasted well.

Next day they rested, sleeping under a rock. They set off again in the evening, leaving the straight temple road and traveling down narrow, winding trails through the dense forest. Before they started they fed again on the wild pig, leaving little behind for the scavenging jackals and crows. Now as night wore on and the moon waned they heard something approaching.

The leopardess stopped, her hair bristling. She bared her teeth uneasily for she could not make out what it was, an odd kind of slithering sound with a rattle and crackling of twigs. It could not be made by a deer, for their kind walk neat and surefooted. It might have been a great snake, yet it seemed to have feet, and a snake does not break down small bushes but slides round or through them. With a snarl she sprang into a tree. The cubs followed her example, but as the strange noise came close, underneath where they perched, the leopardess changed her mind. She jumped down and galloped away, her tail high in the air, with low, worried growls of alarm. The female cub ran at her heels. But the black cub stayed where he was. Fascinated, he waited to watch the strange creature pass by.

Near the trunk of his tree there advanced a long, sinuous body. It was far too broad for a snake, except for the father of all snakes, and it did not move as a snake moves. It crawled along on short legs with stumpy, clawed feet, and it seemed a long time after its snout had gone by that its tail showed its blunt tip. Three creatures like it came behind, then four or five more, while for some distance on either side the cub could hear cracklings and snortings as others pushed through the bushes. A horrible musty, sour odor rose from their bodies. The cub had seen all that he wanted. He wished now to follow his mother, but the long beasts still passed underneath him in threatening procession. He was surrounded by a mass of great shuffling bodies with huge jaws and small, wicked eyes, shining baleful and green in the dim

moonlight. They were crocodiles, a host of crocodiles, which at last had been forced to leave some drought-emptied lake and now followed their leader in search of another moist dwelling.

Their progress was slow, and he grew weary watching them pass. He was worried about his mother, yet feared to descend till the last of the monsters had gone. At last he heard no more sounds of them. He jumped down from the tree and started to hunt for his family.

He called, but his mother did not answer his call. He called again and again, ran aimlessly first one way, then another. The air was heavy and rank with the crocodiles' odor. He thought he heard her far away and galloped to seek her, but when he caught up with the sound he found a strange, pale-coated leopard tearing at some unknown prey, which looked like a large hairless monkey. It snarled, driving him off from its uncanny feast, and he ran away, frightened and lonely.

All night long he hunted for her, going farther and farther, had he but known it, in the opposite direction to hers. At last, by next midday, worn out, he slept in some bushes. He was lost and cut off from his family. From now on he must fend for himself.

5. Noisy Neighbors

For the next few months the black cub led a hard life. He was old and large enough now to look after himself, but like many young creatures of other tribes he would gladly have stayed with his mother. Leopards are fond of their families and keep together. The probability is that, had he not got separated, he would have remained with his mother at least till she found herself a new mate. But now he was all on his own and he had to learn for himself the hard lessons of jungle existence.

He was more than half-grown by now, sleek and handsome, though with just a suspicion of softness and kitten fluffiness still to be found in his coat. His fur was a shining jet black, a very unusual color, for most often so-called "black" leopards are truly a very deep brown on which their tribe's rosette marks show darker yet. The cub had not one trace of any tint other than black. His was a perfect example of melanism.

During those first days after he had lost his family the cub found it desperate work even to keep alive. The dry jungle was all but empty of game, and such as was left was most wary. It was difficult, too, to stalk quietly where the ground was a carpet of dried, rustling leaves and twigs, and each bush rattled out its warning at the faintest touch of his body.

Not only the bushes betrayed him. To his disgust he now found that wherever he wandered a warning went out of his coming. All the birds, the peafowl, plovers and crows, cried beware when they saw him approach. The monkeys coughed and discussed him, following him along their shaking tree roads. The big jungle squirrels whistled, spotted deer belled, and the little red deer barked like dogs. He found it was of little use rushing after these creatures. If he climbed a tree after monkeys he found that they had left it long before he reached its top. The deer that gave the alarm took good care to keep a safe distance between him and them and, fast as he was, with that start it was useless pursuing. He was forced to stalk sun-drowsing lizards. Even insects and old bleaching bones became part of his miserable diet.

He made his home among some rocks where he found a small pool still holding water. He was forced to stay here since he could find drink nowhere else, but he would very gladly have left because of the curious company on which he found he was intruding. This was a troop of sloth bears, the first that the cub had encountered. They were rough and ungainly beasts with uncertain habits and tempers.

The first that he knew of their presence was when he was quenching his thirst the day after he had lost his family. The scent of the water had drawn him from a long distance into a small, gloomy cave where the little pool lay. He was lapping contentedly when he heard something scrape on the rock. He would have dashed out but, before he had time, the cave's opening was blocked by a great shaggy shape which advanced on the water with snorts of intense satisfaction. The cub bared his teeth, his fur bristled, but he sprang away into the shadows, crouching out of harm's way. The beast that had entered was certainly very odd looking. It had a long, blunt, whitish nose and little bright eyes. Its black hair was lengthy and coarse, and its forelegs were bandy and armed with tremendous hooked claws. On its back it appeared to carry a kind of a hump, but this hump unexpectedly detached itself from its perch and came frolicking down to the water. It was a baby sloth bear, which usually traveled in state on its mother's broad shoulders.

Mother and baby were still at their drink when two more bears entered the cave. They snuffled and grunted with joy at the sight of the water, while the leopard cub forced himself into the farthest dim corner. There was scarcely room on the pool's edge for the three bulky creatures, and presently one of the newcomers jostled the other. It replied with a groan of resentment, which rose to a yell as its companion gave it a cuff which tipped it head first into the pool. Then pandemonium broke loose. The mother bear rushed from the cavern with howls of alarm, her young one following her with shrieks like a pig. The two bears that were left settled down to a regular boxing match, both of them roaring and screaming as first one, then the other, was knocked flying into the water. The battle went on for some time with splashing and horrible clamor, though neither seemed much the

worse for it. At last, as if suddenly tiring, they both started sucking up water, pausing only to grumble and groan.

The noise had been really appalling. When the two bears at last went away, seemingly the best of good friends, the black cub still crouched, his heart thumping, quite terrified by the uproar. Yet he soon came to know that this was the bears' usual behavior. They seemed terribly touchy and ready to fight in an instant. The faintest surprise would make them fly into a fury and utter hideous cries. But there seemed too a good deal of humor in their odd antics. They were the clowns of the jungle, and he soon learned they meant him no harm. Only he took good care never again to be caught in the cave when they entered.

Then the rain came. For some days the sky became laden with thick, sullen clouds. Bright lights flickered in the northeast. The air became unbearably still and oppressive. Then heavy and slow the first drops started to fall. Thunder crashed, and the lightning flamed terribly, striking here and there in the forest, blasting great trees. Sheets of water dropped from the sky to spout and splash on the hard earth. The cub sheltered under a rock, his eyes gleaming golden as he stared out in terrified wonder at the dazzling blaze which flashed out again and again. He snarled though his heart throbbed with fear, while above him the rock wallowed like a black, shining whale in the spate of wind-tossed, streaming water.

By morning the sky was swept clear. The jungle had changed overnight. Water dripped everywhere and gleamed in bright pools all over the floor of the forest. The bushes and trees seemed to heave a great sigh of thanksgiving. They stretched gratefully to the sun, which now was no longer a tyrant. The sap started to flow through their veins.

Within a very short while fresh life returned everywhere. The herds of beasts began to drift back to their old grounds. Grass sprouted. A wonderful scent of fresh, happy earth and new growing spread through the air. It rained hard for some hours every day, but the rest of the time the sun shone. Birds sang and the pools became noisy with splashing and croaking of bullfrogs.

The black cub left his rock shelter and his rude neighbors. Thin and hungry, he started away to search for meat for his starved belly. He did not have to go far. In a little glade by a pool he saw a spotted stag grazing, a full-grown stag with long antlers, though as yet these were covered with velvet. The stag was intent on the sprouting fresh blades of grass. Yet every now and again it would shake its horns impatiently, for their soft, blood-filled tips were bumpy with mosquito bites. It was a fine beast such as only a large and veteran leopard would think of attacking, but the cub's heart was set upon food, and as food he determined to get it. Softly he slunk through the bushes, flattened to earth, the tip of his tail gently twitching. Nearer and nearer he crept, while the stag, with its white tail a-flicker, eagerly nibbled, head down. The black cub's whole shape drew together, trembling, tense for the spring. His golden eyes glared without blinking. Five bounds took him up to his prey. A leap

lifted him to its shoulders before it had seen him. The stag jumped away as curved claws closed round its throat, but Black Lightning's weight rode on its withers. It stumbled and fell with a splash among brown, brittle reeds.

For three days the cub rested and fed on the deer he had slain. Then he started again on his travels. The passing months brought him adventures, experience too. His muscles grew strong, and his soft coat glossy and firm. Not often now did he go hungry. He learned how to walk in the way of his kind along paths after rain had fallen, keeping clear of the bushes which made his fur sodden and draggled. He learned to crouch low to the ground when seeking for game, for thus he could best get an unhampered view under the branches. He took note of the way other creatures lived in the jungle: where deer were to be found at the different hours of day and night; how to wait in ambush for monkeys on their own trails. There was nothing to dispute the rule of his tribe in the forest, for the bears and elephants, the only beasts stronger than they, always left them alone. There was no rivalry between them. The elephants fed on leaves, branches, and fruit from the trees. The bears ate insects, fruit, flowers, roots, and honey when they could find it. One dangerous enemy only the leopards had, and that was man.

It was natural that, in the pride of his young, splendid strength, he should grow overconfident. When he found that most things in the forest feared him and the rest gave him respectful room the black leopard became proud and reckless. When he felt in the mood he chased for the sheer love of chasing. His youthful progress might be marked through the woods by the flapping and screeching of peafowl, the scramble of terrified monkeys, the dash of stampeding deer, none of which he had any real intention of hurting and would have been wiser to leave to their own occupations.

But pride was to suffer a fall. It chanced that one blazing midday, when he would have been better asleep in the shade of a rock, Black Lightning was prowling silently through a small swamp. He halted to crouch in some grass, for out in a little glade's center he beheld a remarkable creature. It lay basking in warm, sloppy mud, and it was not like anything else that the young black leopard had met.

It was about as long as a porcupine, though not as fat. It was covered with muddy gray hair, with two great eyes and ears at one end, and a moist, grayish nose at the other. But perhaps the most odd thing about it was that for all its small size it sprouted a pair of immense black crescent-shaped horns.

Whatever it might be, Black Lightning decided to stalk it, out of pure devilment. He had eaten not too long ago and was by no means hungry. Eyes full of bright curiosity, his silent pads delicately lifting and pressing the ground, he approached to within charging distance. The gray animal did not take any notice of him. Its big eyes under their long, soft lashes, were partly closed, as if it drowsed. Black Lightning flattened and mustered himself for his spring, his paws rippling, his long tail jerking. Suddenly he launched himself headlong at the gray beast.

The strange animal uttered a snort which grew into a tremendous bellow, surprisingly loud for its size. As Black Lightning straddled and clawed it, he found himself being lifted up from the ground. A terrific disturbance was going on in the mud pool, from which a bulky wet shape came surging up behind his quarry.

It was all too odd altogether. The black leopard snarled and rebounded from his prey. The great buffalo, which had been wallowing at its ease, floundered up out of its hole and rushed at him with its head down, bellowing angrily. The sight of those sharp, widespread horns made Black Lightning run for his life, the bull close behind him. After that he treated all buffaloes with respect, nor was he so ready to chase anything that he saw.

He was full grown now but as yet found no place to settle, no regular beat in the jungle such as most leopards have. He wandered along on his own, through the deep forests that cover the southeastern part of the island. Now and again he met other ones of his kind. But although sometimes he fought with a male which resented him in its domain, and sometimes dallied with a female, he made no stay in one place, and he took no mate.

6. The Elephant Herd

So passed another dry season, and the time of rain came again. Black Lightning sprawled on a rock in the afternoon sunshine, drowsily watching the comical goings-on of some bears. He saw a mother bear gallop wildly downhill, sliding and clattering over the wet earth and boulders, while her little one rode like a jockey, bumping and jerking but never losing his seat. Another bear dashed after her, perhaps her husband. Finding his progress too slow, or annoyed by the slippery foothold, this one rolled himself into a ball and went bouncing and rolling wildly after the first. From the trees below there sounded puffings and gruntings, blowings and wheezings, as other bears snuffled and gulped the white ants out of their hills. A curious kind of a humming noise could be heard too, which was made as they put their paws in their mouths, sucking the pads which had grown sore with much hard digging.

Black Lightning got up and stretched himself. He looked over the jungle from his rock peak, across the tops of the trees, now gay with green leaves and flowers. He saw in one place branches shaking and decided to go and explore. Those branch shakings were made by elephants, and he knew very well that under cover of their noisy company he might easily get close to game.

He ran down the slope through the rocks and the great dim trees where the sun's rays came slanting and the bears dug and delved in the anthills. Then along the floor of the jungle he trotted until he saw the herd. Half a dozen elephants stood there, four of them full-grown beasts and two young ones not much bigger than Shetland ponies and nearly as hairy. The bull of the herd was a fine creature, almost ten feet high and with curving, beautiful tusks. His and his cows' and calves' hides were covered with dusty red mud from the lake in which they had spent most of the last night bathing. They looked like great sandstone boulders among the green jungle, with their rounded backs and domed heads. Now they stood placidly tearing down bouquets of succulent leaves and stuffing these into their mouths, or reaching high up for a fruit called "jungle apple," which is full of applelike pulp. If they came on a sweet, sappy tree, too wide to cram into their mouths, they would break it into short lengths and roll these backward and forward under their feet till the bark came off and the stringy inside could be chewed. Their little eyes beamed with contentment while, like thunder, their tummies rumbled in happy digestion. For many months they had been harassed, with little to eat in the jungle and clashes with man and man's weapons when his crops tempted them into thieving. But here, in this faraway place and this season of plenty, they had ample food and a quiet life, which was all that they wanted.

Black Lightning chose a sunny place against a tree. He rolled on his back on the warm ground, watching the glad, harmless monsters. There were no deer in sight and he could not be bothered to go on a chase after monkeys. In fact, he was not really hungry. Lazily he lay watching the great flapping ears of the elephants swing to and fro, to and fro, while their tufted tails whisked at the flies. They paid no attention to him, though when one of the little ones wandered off in his direction his mother smacked it with her trunk and drew it back close to her body.

The bull dusted a wisp of grass against his round, ponderous foreleg. One of the worst things that can happen to an elephant is to get an ant up his nose. There is such a lot of his nose; and some kinds of ants not only bite but sting too, so that it is quite easy to understand how much an elephant fears them. That is one of the reasons why an elephant always dusts everything carefully before carrying it to his jaws.

The bull pushed the tussock of grass into his mouth. He chewed it between his broad teeth and started to march from the glade. The rest of his herd trailed behind him, and, with nothing better to do, Black Lightning followed him too. The elephants were moving off to the lake for their evening bathe.

Black Lightning stared at a high branch where a splendid peacock sat squalling. Its feathers shone like bronze and sapphires, and it miaowed like an enormous cat. Black hornbills —with big gold crowns and beaks as large and bright as

bananas—went flying ahead of the elephants, laughing like human folk. The leopard made one half-hearted leap after a hare which darted from under his paws, but let it escape in the bushes. Then they came to the edge of the lake, and he sat down to watch again.

This lake looked very different from that desolate sea of baked mud which he and his mother had visited when he was a half-grown cub. It stretched full and serene and silver, with much of its surface covered with flat lotus leaves and their big red and white water lilies. All kinds of birds swam and flew and waded about and around it, and across its still surface were scattered the dark shapes of crocodiles.

Black Lightning often came to this lake of an evening to drink and see what game was there, but tonight something struck him as different. Like most other animals, he was no great hand at counting, but he had more than enough wit to see there were more elephants here than he had noticed before. Usually there was only the one small herd bathing— the herd he had just followed down. But tonight there were two other herds, so that in all perhaps more than twenty elephants bathed in the lake.

He watched his herd go wading out, joyously squealing and squirting water about them, deeper and deeper till the young ones were almost submerged and only the tops of their little trunks and heads showed. He knew they would stay there for hours, but he had eaten well not long ago and felt in no hurry to move. He found a dry, warm patch of earth and curled up to sleep.

He woke to hear the herd passing on its way back to the forest. He felt sleepy and drowsed off again, but awoke not long after and sat up listening intently. What was that? The elephants were coming back. Why should they come back now? It was their usual habit to return to the jungle some time toward morning, there to doze and feed in desultory fashion until the time came to rest through the midday hours. What could have sent them back to the lake, now while the moon was still shining?

The elephants had halted not far away from his bed. He could sense that they were disturbed. Some of them grumbled and growled. But, although with each other they could converse in this fashion, it was impossible for him to discover the cause of their restlessness. Presently, however, they settled down quietly to wait for the sun to come up.

In the morning, as the mist from the lake cleared away, flight after flight of wild fowl on glittering wings returned to the rosy-hued water. Black Lightning rose, stretched, and yawned. He saw that the two other elephant herds still stood among the trees by the lake's side. What could be the reason for this? It was strange, very strange, for during the heat of the day the elephants love the most hidden part of the forest. Their habit was to start moving toward it long before the sun rose. But during his long sleep Black Lightning had become hungry. Whatever worried the elephants was no concern of his. He decided to leave them now.

He killed, early that morning, a young and tasty wild pig that came running toward him as if it were being pursued.

He cleaned his long whiskers and carefully groomed his jet coat, drank at a stream and curled himself for a nap through the long, hot noon. He woke, sitting up with a start. What now? What had made him awake, feeling full of suspicion? He stared round about him, tail twitching, his round ears cocked. Then in a flash he slipped silently down from his rock. Something had shown for a moment alongside a tree, and that something he knew was a man.

So far in his travels Black Lightning had had very little close acquaintance with men. Yet from a distance he had managed to study them. He had lain close to their villages, watched them at work in their fields, trailed them sometimes for pure sport as they followed a jungle path, little dreaming of the great beast that prowled so silent on their heels. But, though instinct and in some part his mother's teaching both warned him to avoid them whenever possible, he regarded men indifferently, not classing them as deadly enemies any more than he classed them as prey.

Therefore he did not run far but crouched to see what this man was going to do. He did not have to wait long. Softly and cautiously the brown man came climbing over the top of the rock which the leopard had only just left. He was moving down now, and Black Lightning glided away like a swift-moving shadow. He ran for a hundred yards and then turned sharp right in the direction for which he was heading when he first met the intruder. He had not progressed far when he snarled and swerved violently back. Another man stood in the bushes and, thirty bounds on, yet another.

He turned back toward the lake. No men were there. At any rate, there had been no men near when he had left it. And the men he had met had all seemed to be coming from the other direction. But when he got there he found the elephants huddled together uneasily. The three herds had drawn closer together, and they were not feeding. They were flapping their sensitive ears and waving their trunks. Something was in the wind, and their trunks told them part of the story. The bulls muttered and rocked to and fro, stamping out now and again in short, nervous rushes. The cows squealed and kept their calves close against their bodies and legs. So they stood until midafternoon.

Then the tapping began. *Tap-tap*, very faintly—so faint that it might have been the furtive sound of an insect or a little bird at its work. *Tap-tap* again. The bull elephants' ears stuck out stiffly, quivering, listening hard. *Tap-tap* once more. The cows swung up their curling trunks. The bulls strode toward the sound. Black Lightning stood tense and alert. What could this be?

The bulls had halted, confused. The tapping had sounded in front of them on this side of the lake. Now it sounded behind them too, on the lake's other side. Very gently it sounded, not really alarming, just a quiet *tap-tap-tapping* of wood against echoing wood.

The three elephant herds drew closer and closer together. A young bull led out his family of cow and calf, starting away for the trees on the lake's far side. But within ten minutes they trotted back, puzzled and angry. He had found something there which had stopped them from getting away.

Black Lightning walked over to see what had made them return. He walked for a quarter of a mile before he heard any more tapping. Then it began again softly, and he saw a fresh pair of elephants moving toward him through the swaying green branches. *Tap-tap, tap-tap.* It was very close now, but not loud. He bounded ahead, then halted suddenly, crouching. He saw a man slowly advance, a stick in his hand. So they were here too! He ran silently back, then along the line of the beaters; jinked and darted toward them, belly to ground. But a man stood right in his way, and on each side of him, only a few paces off, Black Lightning saw other men, and more men, more men in a line, wherever he ran.

All were moving steadily forward, some with sticks, some with guns in their hands. And the *tap-tap-tapping* went on. Away on the lake's distant side, Black Lightning could hear like an echo the faint sound of those other men beating. He turned round and slunk back to the elephants.

And now the elephants started to trumpet and stamp. They squealed as they crowded together, ears and trunks waving, while a cloud of dust rose all about them. Suddenly, as at a signal, the whole mass stampeded away, away from the lake, the little ones wildly skedaddling after their mothers. Black Lightning stared round him, then cantered along after them. There was no other way out. The lake blocked his way to the south. East and west the beaters advanced. There was only one way to go—north.

7. The Great Hunt

As he followed the elephant herds Black Lightning caught sight of a number of other animals running away from the beaters. Spotted deer galloped away, paying little attention to him except to swerve and fly faster still. A sambhur stag, large as a horse, with rough mane and heavy, pronged horns, raced by with its hind and fawn. Wild pigs scuttled off, grunting, the boars with their curved tusks gleaming, and little thin tails carried high. Troops of monkeys hurtled and fled through the trees.

For a few miles he kept with the elephants, which, after their first dash of panic, had settled down to a fast, swinging stride they seemed to intend to keep up. But Black Lightning wanted to know what was going on in the rear. Had those men stopped or were they still in pursuit? He climbed up a tree to crouch in a high and convenient bough.

Half an hour passed, then he heard a crackle of twigs. Yes, there was a man coming toward him. He still held a stick but he was not tapping any more. To right and left the leopard heard other men moving. He ran head-first down the tree trunk and went on after the herd.

They halted during the night. It seemed that at last they

had left the beaters behind. Black Lightning began to look round for something to eat. The excitement had made him hungry. He managed to pounce on a hare, but that was not enough for his appetite. A deer called somewhere in the darkness, and he stalked it across a dim glade.

The deer saw him first and dashed away through the trees. Black Lightning raced after it, was close on its betraying white tail, when he caught a strong whiff of man-smell. He saw a little fire burning, men sitting round it, their faces aglow from its blaze. Another fire shone through the trees not very far off, and another one beyond that. Why, all through the woods there were fires, like little bright eyes! He turned back while the deer went rushing on.

It was outside his powers to reason what all this might mean. All he knew was that round him and the elephants stretched a great army of men. He did not know what they were after, but his natural caution kept him from trying to make a break through their ranks. Besides, there was always that way to the north still open. Had he been an older and more experienced animal, he might have guessed where that way led, why all creatures except the elephants were allowed to escape through the cordon of men.

That night the elephants never kept still for long. They were thirsty, but there seemed no water here for them. Now that immediate danger no longer appeared to threaten, they had separated again into their different herds. After feeding uneasily for a few hours they were on the move northward again long before midnight.

The black leopard went with them. He knew, even if they did not know, the danger hemming them in. Sometimes he traveled in front of them, sometimes behind, but he was never long out of earshot of the noises that elephants make— the rustling and breaking of branches, the smacking of leathery ears and occasional trumpetings.

Dawn found them marching through a forest of enormous trees, trees which had been standing here for a thousand years, perhaps longer. Their straight stems stretched a hundred feet toward the sky, and where their tops met they made a new world of their own, a world of bright flowers and bees, of rarest, most beautiful orchids, fruits and fresh, sparkling air, which the monkeys and gold-crowned hornbills claimed as their kingdom.

Through the floor of this world in the sky long beams of sunshine came slanting, piercing the gloom underneath. The elephants moved in and out of these brilliant shafts, pressing on after their leader toward a remembered river where they might drink and bathe. Beside them paced a black shadow— a black leopard with golden eyes.

They halted at evening so that the young ones might rest. The little beasts had started lagging, though for mile after mile they had kept up gamely enough, trotting along with their small trunks twined round their mothers' tails. Now the mother cows began to grumble. If the herd kept on at this rate, they grunted, *they* would have to be left behind. Their calves must be fed. They could not keep up the pace.

They had quitted the primeval forest. Now they stood in

a dried watercourse, the bed of a onetime river, where the trees formed a tall green tunnel knitted with creepers. From these creepers huge beanpods dangled, six feet in length and five or six inches across. The elephants fed on fresh branches and grass and, having no water, took sand baths. They did this by scooping up sand in a curl of their trunks and casting it over their bodies till they were quite covered. It discouraged insects and flies.

Black Lightning was sleepy and dozed. He was in no mood to go hunting. He felt anxious and worried by the strange things going on around him. He wished he could get right away, away from the elephants and, above all, from the men. Perhaps now, though, they had managed to leave the men far behind.

He awoke again in the dark and decided to go and investigate. The whole jungle seemed full of elephants. Surely far more were here now than the three herds with which he had started. Wherever he went they were standing about in the blackness, grumbling and restless. The air was heavy with the smell of their droppings and the bruised leaves torn down and trampled. Well, he had had quite enough of them. He would go away now, far away.

He started to go to the west. But no, the men were still there. He soon came on the line of their fires, closer together now than they had been last night. He dared not attempt to break through, for he heard the sound of their voices softly talking. He turned back eastward. Less than a mile away he found that line of fires too. He began to lope through the forest, hidden, on a parallel course to the fireline. He was heading back to the south. There must be a break somewhere in that line of fires, or perhaps it would suddenly end.

And then, straight ahead, a most awful uproar exploded. Without any warning, blood-curdling yells and whoops roared from hundreds of human throats. Drums rattled and boomed. Guns banged. Black Lightning jumped a clear three feet in the air. Every one of his hairs stood on end, and his yellow eyes opened wide with surprise and terror. He leaped round and galloped back, where he heard the elephants screaming and roaring. Their huge feet pounded the ground as they wheeled and tore for the north; and as they stampeded fresh shouts and drummings broke out, keeping pace with them. Torches waved too, flickering and leaping in long lines on either side. If they swerved to the right torches flared into their little terrified eyes. Guns flashed and crashed over their heads. If they turned left the same thing happened. Yet, ahead, it was silent and dark. Sanctuary awaited them there. And so they raced on always northward, down an ever narrowing avenue made by men and their terrible fire.

The black leopard soon outstripped the elephant herd that he knew. He speeded ahead in great bounds, leaping over bushes and rocks, his tail high in a vibrating curve. He passed more elephants rushing madly, squealing and trumpeting, while behind and on each side of them the frightful commotion swelled, the lights glared and danced through the trees. He raced blindly ahead, intent on escaping the noise and the humans. So it was he arrived at full speed in a mighty enclosure, whose widespreading wings, funnel shaped, had imprisoned the panicking herds.

This trap was built in a great circle, made of tree trunks sunk in the ground, buttressed and battened together. The first elephants pounded across it to burst through its opposite side, where the shadowy barrier stood some dozen feet high. Their leader had all but crashed into it when torches flared all round the ring as men plucked them out of small fires and brandished them furiously. The bull elephant roared, but he flinched as torches were flung in his face and dozens of long, fresh-peeled rods were thrust at him by the crowd of men outside the fence. Had he led his herd on in its assault they could have smashed through it to freedom as if the tough timbers were matchwood. But, daunted, he stopped, then swung away on a fresh charge.

A howl from the great host of men had greeted the elephants' rush. Now another howl sounded as they caught sight of the black leopard, mad with fear and rage in their trap, crouching and snarling in the lurid glow of the flames. They had not bargained for him and would willingly have let him go, for their only intention was to catch the wild elephants to tame and train them. A headman ran to the chief in charge of the hunt.

"The leopard will frighten our noosers and the elephants too. What shall we do with him?" he asked.

The chief stood up on his platform, close by the gate of the trap, from which he could see the whole course of the elephants' catching. Down there, inside the arena, he saw the black leopard crouched while the elephants milled all about him.

"Bring me my rifle," he ordered.

One of his men touched his arm. "*Aiya,* if that leopard is caught he will obtain a high price in a circus or zoo. Black leopards are very rare. Surely there is some way to take him alive."

The chief considered. He called an old bearded hunter, a Vedda, one of the aboriginal tribesmen who live in Ceylon's great forests. He said some quick words to the man, who nodded his head, not forward but, in his folks' fashion, from side to side.

The elephant catchers' leader shouted from where he sat on the neck of a great decoy cow. He had just given orders that the heavy bars should be let down to close the trap's entrance.

"Oh, *Hamadoru,*" he shouted, "the gate is shut now, and my noosemen are ready to enter. But they will not go in while that black devil-cat crouches there."

"Go then and try quickly," the chief told the old jungle man. "If he is not caught within ten minutes he must be shot."

8. In Captivity

Black Lightning had made one attempt to get over the barrier. He had tried a splendid leap and clawed hold of its top. But a villager without much sense had thrown a torch straight in his face. Black Lightning had fallen back, swearing, his whiskers and eyebrows singed. Although he had been terrified he was in a mood now to fight.

"Fool, why did you do that?" the villager's neighbors complained, pressing sideways and back from that part of the barrier which the leopard was facing. They were scared of the leopard, which they half feared was some jungle devil. Who had ever seen a *black* leopard, and one which came galloping among an elephant herd? "Better to have let him go. He will only cause trouble here."

"Then I will put an end to him," another man shouted. He elbowed his way to the front, bearing a gun and thinking himself a great hero. But the chief's jungle hunter and some of his men, dark, silent men like himself, had arrived in the crowd.

"Stand aside. It is the chief's order," they told him. They carried a net. Two of them climbed on the barrier and worked their way quietly along it.

The elephants still rushed to and fro in frenzied attempts to escape. Some of them were growing tired and had formed a ring in the trap's center, their young ones in safety inside it. But the others led by the bull kept making ferocious charges, halted each time by the torches and white, pointing sticks. Black Lightning squatted close to the ground, watching their efforts, taking care to keep out of the way of their earth-shaking feet. Now and again he glared back over his shoulders, tail lashing, ears lying flat, to snarl at the men by the fence. But among all the uproar, the banging, the booms, and the shouting, he did not notice the two little dark-bodied men who poised on the barrier above him, the net in their hands.

Something swooped and fell over his head. He sprang up, tried to tear it away, then rolled on his back, his hindlegs kicking like fury. But the net was all over his body. His paws and his teeth tangled in it, and, although he tried to chew through it, there were too many tough squares of cord. When he was properly enmeshed the men ran to attach a rope with a hook at its end. They dragged him away, a helpless, furious bundle, close to the arena's side. He struggled and struggled, but another net covered the first. Soon he lay exhausted and panting, watching the fate of the elephants.

The gate had opened to let the decoy beasts come in. These were tamed elephants, trained to help in catching the wild ones. A large and stately cow led them, her driver astride her neck, and eight more followed her, each with a man

riding it. She made her way unhurriedly across to the bull, the herd's leader, who advanced to meet her and clasped his trunk around hers. The cow wore a pleased look in her eye as if she enjoyed the treacherous work she was doing.

She ranged up close to the bull and from under her belly a man crept out with a noose. He waited his chance till the wild bull lifted one foot, then slipped the loop over his leg. Before the bull knew he had been caught the noose was drawn tight, and he found himself being hauled off from the rest of his comrades. The decoy cow had the rope's other end attached to her collar. As she dragged off the unwilling bull, one of her companion decoys, an enormous tusker, came to her aid and pushed him along with his forehead. The poor beast could not help himself. He caught at a tree, but the tusker tore loose his grip. He was pulled roaring away and shackled by all four feet to four sturdy trees. There he kicked and struggled and bellowed, throwing himself on the ground, contorting his body into the oddest positions. But it was all of no use.

The same fate befell all the others. One by one the soft, pliant nooses were slipped on their legs and they were hauled slowly away to be bound to strong trees. The noosemen worked bravely and quickly, but if ever they were in danger from an angry elephant's trunk a decoy beast would step in between and ward off the blow. The decoys seemed to need little direction; indeed, they appeared to take a real pleasure and interest in helping to catch their wild kinsmen.

At last all the big elephants had been tied up to trees.

Some of them still wrestled and fought to break free. They picked at the knots of their bonds with their trunks. They doubled their heads underneath them and balanced themselves on their forelegs, striving to tear their uplifted hind-legs loose. They wriggled and rolled and screamed, as no one who has not seen would believe an elephant could do. Others lay panting pathetically with tears rolling down their great cheeks. Again and again they threw dust over their bodies. They pushed their trunks into their throats, sucking water back out of their stomachs, with which they sprayed themselves freely. Soon almost all of them had made for themselves slushy hollows in which they lay covered with mud.

Only the little calves still ran free in the trap. They followed their mothers, to stand by their big, helpless bodies, screaming and dashing to attack anyone who came near them. When they were driven away they ran to the other cows, who each caressed them in turn. The men who worked in the arena laughed at their antics and fed them with soft stalks of plantain and sugar cane, which the little beasts snatched and ate greedily even while they were tearing with rage. These men were not really cruel. They needed the wild elephants to work in the forests and fields. They knew very well that the beasts which lay groaning so wretchedly would within a very few months become docile and willing, helping to fell trees, haul timber, even to march in procession with the chief's *howdahs* borne on their backs. Soon each elephant had its keeper, who fed it on fresh, juicy leaves and escorted it, tied to a decoy, down to the nearby river to bathe and drink.

While all this was going on the black leopard lay helpless and raging. The gaily clad men and women who came flocking into the enclosure to look at the captive monsters kept well away from him.

"Look at that fierce black demon. See his teeth!" the men shouted, while the maidens glanced at him with scared brown eyes, ready to run for their lives if he did but move. But Black Lightning was wrapped in a tight, cramped cocoon in the nets. He could not stir even his tail.

A boy stood staring longer than anyone else. He seemed completely fascinated by the leopard's unwinking gold eyes.

"*Aiyo,* what a terrible creature. How I fear him!" he whispered.

"Nay, little one, do not be afraid." A Buddhist monk with shaved head and pale, lemon-hued robe took the boy's hand, standing with him to watch poor Black Lightning. His eyes were gentle and kind. "Remember that teaching which I have imparted to you. This poor beast is brother to us. Perchance in his next life he will be born as a man. Or perhaps, in his last existence, as a man he performed some ill deed which doomed him to return to earth in this animal's shape."

"Oh, oh," the boy murmured, staring first at the monk, whose little disciple he was, and then at the leopard as if with a new understanding. His big eyes held a wondering sympathy. "Oh, my teacher, what evil deed did he do?"

The monk smiled. "That I know not, my pupil. Yet it is

foolish to fear or bear hatred to any poor beast. They are pilgrims like us down the long road of many rebirths. Therefore the Lord Buddha taught we should treat every creature with kindness."

And he led the boy off, but the boy looked back often at Black Lightning bound in the nets.

Some time in the morning they brought a rough cage made of stout bars well lashed together. One end was open, and they slipped a rope through the other, so that they could haul the leopard inside it. Then the open end was closed up, and through the bars of the cage a bold hunter cautiously hacked through some of the meshes of the net, leaving it to the black leopard to squirm his way clear of his bonds. This he succeeded in doing after some desperate wriggling and clawing. He crouched in the low, narrow cage, his fur all ruffled, his eyes glaring out at the men who moved across his view.

Toward evening four men came and lifted the cage on long poles. They carried it off on their shoulders, out of the great enclosure where the captive elephants stood or lay tied to their trees. Some were already placidly eating the food given them by their keepers.

They did not feed Black Lightning yet, though somebody had given him water. He struck at the hand which thrust the gift through the bars, upsetting the bowl. He would not have drunk of it anyway. He was too moved by anger and fear to seek anything but escape.

The four men carried the cage through the excited crowd, laying it down with a grunt in the back of a bullock cart. The draft oxen stamped and jingled the bells around their necks, trying to break away as they caught the scent of the leopard.

"Steady, steady!" the driver soothed them. "Oh, my brother," he shouted, "are you ready to start? It grows late."

A struggle with squealings and laughter was going on now as another cart was loaded up. Black Lightning could not see, but into that cart they were pushing one of the little calf elephants. It was being sent off with the leopard to a town to be sold to a circus, but before it was lifted on board it grabbed everything it could reach with its small agile trunk. It protested most bitterly about being dragged off from its mother, but presently the two carts got started. They rumbled and squeaked down a bumpy track through the forest.

Black Lightning had scarcely stirred in his little barred prison. As they rattled away from the dust and the noise of the crowd he became aware that night was falling again. He felt the air cooling, heard the parrots' shrill evening cries as they wheeled high and free through the sky. The world was growing shadowy and hushed to silence. It was *his* hour now that was coming, the hour at which night after night he had sallied out, stalking his prey, making the forest afraid with his hunting song.

Carefully he reached out a paw, hooking his claws around a bar, testing its strength. The bar creaked and bent just a little as he pulled on it with his full weight. But it was of strong, springy timber and would not give much or break. He tried each one. None of them yielded.

Pushing his face close against the side of his cage, he tried chewing the lashings which held the bars in their places. But, although he managed to bite through the tough, fibrous creepers, the bars had been nailed down as well. He could not get out. In the narrow space he hurled himself at the cage's end. It was no good. Panting and bruised, with raw places rubbed in his hide, which had been so silky and sleek, he lay down to see what might come.

9. The Circus

The carters did not keep on when the sun had set. They turned loose their hump-backed white bulls by the side of the track, where their shining bells told their masters just where they were as they grazed, besides warning wild beasts away. The men lit a fire and crouched beside it, cooking their rice, before they rolled up in their blankets to go to sleep.

But Black Lightning did not sleep. Hour after hour he heard the night sounds of the jungle: the long, dreary calls of the jackals, the unending song of the crickets. He heard a deer cry in the distance, then the bell of a sambhur stag, sharp and clear as a trumpet blast. All the sweet, wild odors he knew floated into his nostrils, but he was shut here in his prison, among them but cut off completely.

Next morning the carters started early, through the pale mists which covered the forest. They gave Black Lightning some water, and this time he lapped it up thirstily, for he had not drunk for more than forty-eight hours. They threw him some raw deer meat too, and he grabbed this and tore at it, snarling.

"What a bloodthirsty brute!" said the carters, who had

never been chased day and night with torches and guns, then caught in a net, then pushed in a little tight cage without any food.

That day they rolled onto a road and drove slowly along it under the blazing sun. They followed this road for two days. The cart had a caravan roof of palm thatch, which sheltered the cage from the worst heat, though inside it was breathlessly hot and swarms of flies buzzed in and out. But it did not save the leopard from the crowds that followed the carts whenever they passed through a village, shouting and pushing to see him.

On the evening of the third day they came to a town. There the crowd redoubled, and some brute prodded Black Lightning with a long stick. The leopard growled and tore at its end with his teeth while the callous crowd roared their applause. But the bullock carts rumbled and creaked away from the street into a station yard, where the cage was hauled out and dumped on one of the platforms.

The little elephant too was heaved out, struggling and bawling. A man had traveled with it to look after it in the cart. He fed it on plantain stems, and the waiting passengers gave it bananas and sugar cane. The man threw some stale meat to Black Lightning, but the passengers did not feed him. They stood at a safe distance and stared.

When the train came in the animals were pushed on board in one of the freight cars. The train was bound for Colombo, the great port down in the south, where the man in charge of them had been told to sell them to a circus. The young elephant did not enjoy the long journey; nor did Black Lightning, but he kept silent about it.

At Colombo station two men were waiting to meet them. One was a fat Indian with a big, waxed mustache, gold teeth and rings on his fingers; the other, a husky young Negro who wore a big white cowboy hat. The fat Indian was the circus owner and ringmaster. He had been warned by telegram to expect the leopard and elephant. The Negro was called Buddy Buck. He was a heavyweight boxing champion who had started life in America.

The circus proprietor looked over the elephant calf. He stooped down as far as his enormous stomach would let him to peer into the black leopard's cage.

"The elephant will be useful to us in the circus," he told the big Negro. "He can wear a little clown's hat. The audiences always laugh when they see such a comical creature. But the leopard, I do not see how we can use him."

"But, Boss, he's a mighty fine beast," said the Negro, who preferred anything strong and fierce. "Say, couldn't you use him in the performing animals' act, 'long with the tigers an' lions?" He was stooping too, staring admiringly at Black Lightning.

"Buck, you don't know much. Black leopards can never be tamed. Everybody knows that. No. He is worth just a little price to put in the menagerie. I will offer fifty rupees."

"His hide's worth better'n that, Boss," the Negro argued, standing up and lighting a very long black cigar. "Leastways, it was before they knocked it about in that cage. Tell you what, Boss, Lena the lioness is gettin' too old for her job on the Wall. How 'bout me takin' him on instead of ol' Lena?"

The Indian laughed. "Buck, man, you're crazy! You don't know what you're talking about. This leopard is not like old Lena. He is wild. He is vicious, I tell you."

"You buy him, Boss," urged the Negro. "It's my risk anyways, ain't it?"

So after a great deal of talk the Indian paid four hundred rupees for the small elephant and the leopard. He handed the roll of money to the man who had come with the animals, who tucked it carefully into a fold of his sarong and salaamed and sat down on the platform to wait for a train going north. The Negro called up some porters, who carried the leopard's cage to a ramshackle truck with CASTRO'S IMPERIAL CIRCUS painted in big letters on it. They pushed the baby elephant safely on board. The Indian drove while the Negro sat in the back to look after the animals. He talked a lot to the elephant and a little bit to Black Lightning, squatting and staring in at those bright, gold eyes.

"You sure look mean, buddy," he told him. "But just you wait till you an' me gets roarin' around on the ol' bike. Whoopee, boy, we'll sure show 'em!"

Now, besides being a heavyweight boxer (take on all comers), Buddy Buck rode in a terrible thing in the fair attached to the circus. It was called the Wall of Death and consisted of a wooden cylinder, about twenty-five feet high and fifteen feet in diameter. Buddy Buck rode around its inside on a red motor bicycle with no silencer on its exhaust. As he roared around and around the smooth surface, high off the ground and hanging on like a fly, the audience yelled with excitement. Every moment they expected (and some of them secretly hoped, it is sad to say) to see Buddy go crashing head over heels to the bottom. But, although it looked terribly dangerous, it was not really so bad. The speed seemed much more than it was, and centrifugal force kept Buddy safe in the way that water stays in a glass when somebody whirls it around quickly.

When he had ridden around for a while by himself, shooting up to the cylinder's rim and down again to its bottom, Buddy Buck would invite anyone from the onlookers to accompany him on his pillion. Sometimes he got volunteers, but if he did not somebody out of the circus would pretend to be one of the audience. He would whisk them away for a ride around the terrible wall, and after that came the big moment, the climax of his show. He told the crowd he was going to ride with a lioness sitting behind him. It had taken him some time to get Lena accustomed to this, but she was inclined to put up with most things after ten years of circus life. He did not have very great difficulty in persuading her to sit still with her paws on his shoulders, and the audience roared while he drove at first slowly then faster and faster around the tall Wall of Death.

But now Lena was getting old. Buddy Buck suspected that racing around in small circles made her feel bilious. Once or twice she had nearly come off, keeping herself on the pillion only by sinking her claws in his shoulders, which were luckily very well padded. He felt she was due for a rest, and for some months he had been looking round for some creature to take her place. Black Lightning seemed just what he needed.

10. The Wall of Death

The truck arrived at the fairground, which was in a small open place surrounded by streets lined with bazaars and rickety houses. It was deep in the heart of the native quarter, the *pettah*. Very few white men came to it except a few sailors or tourists out on a spree. The circus proprietor gave orders for the young elephant to be taken away to a corner where he had two full-grown beasts picketed. Black Lightning's cage was carried into a tent, and out of it he was prodded into another that was only a trifle larger. This was the circus menagerie, where for a few cents people came to stare at the animals. No performing beasts were kept here. The lions and tigers lived in their traveling wagons. Its inhabitants were a few monkeys, a mangy old bear, a mongoose, and a long-nosed, scaly anteater, which spent most of its time rolled into a round, horny ball. It was a poor, miserable show.

The monkeys started to scream as soon as the leopard arrived. His cage was down on the floor, which was damp dirty grass, in a dark corner, with the mongoose's box on its top. The tent smelled abominably. It was never properly cleaned, and the animals' wretched food was allowed to decay in their cages. The attendant gave Black Lightning some water and a hunk of old buffalo meat that was mostly gristle and bone.

All through the afternoon and evening people came in to see the animals. The black leopard was a great attraction, especially when he snarled, as he did very often, showing his long white teeth. The fat circus proprietor came in after dark and stood under the paraffin lamp around which scores of insects were fluttering. He was sweating, for the night was stuffy and hot, but he looked rather pleased when he saw the amount of attention the leopard was drawing.

"Perhaps after all he will not be too bad an investment," he told Buddy Buck, whose Wall of Death had been making a horrible noise only a few yards away. The young Negro was wearing the jersey with red and blue stripes and the crash helmet he used on his desperate rides around the Wall.

"You wait, Boss. I'm gonna make friends wit' him; get him to ride on my bike. Gee, I'll start workin' on him tomorrow. We'll tear 'em apart."

"You're crazy, I tell you, Buck," the proprietor said. "You'll get torn into pieces. That will be all that will happen."

Black Lightning was glad when at last the people stopped coming. He curled up as well as he could and slept, though the monkeys whimpered, the mongoose never stopped pattering to and fro overhead, and the old bear rattled its chain and snored very loudly. In the morning Buddy Buck brought him a fresh piece of meat. Black Lightning snatched at it and nearly got him by the hand.

"Steady, bo', steady," Buck soothed him; but Black Lightning only growled and crouched glaring into his eyes.

"Guess I'll have to try some other way," Buddy Buck admitted after three days had passed and he had not made any progress in taming the leopard. He said nothing to the proprietor, but he was a determined young man and he fancied the picture of Black Lightning seated behind him, powerful and sleek, while he raced around the Wall of Death. Next time he brought food for the leopard it had some white stuff sprinkled on it. It was fresh meat again, and Black Lightning swallowed it greedily, paying no heed to the powder. After that he began to feel rather stupid and drowsy. Presently Buddy came in with some men who dragged his cage out and wheeled it along on a trolley inside the round Wall of Death. He growled when they tipped him out, and he aimed a halfhearted blow at the Negro, who was wearing thick leather gauntlets as well as his padded jersey and helmet.

"Come on, bo'. You'll be okay," Buddy told Black Lightning. He had the wild-animal tamer with him, armed with a whip and a stout, much-clawed kitchen chair.

They heaved Black Lightning onto the motor-bicycle's pillion, sitting him squarely down with his paws resting on Buddy's shoulders. Then they pushed the machine around the enclosure two or three times without starting up its engine. Black Lightning sat in a stupor, his eyes almost closed. The drug which Buddy Buck had administered had made him half conscious. He scarcely knew what they were doing.

"All right. Let's go," Buddy Buck said and kicked the engine into action. Dimly Black Lightning heard its hideous roar. He felt himself whirling along, but he was so dazed that he simply held on tight to the Negro's shoulders. After a half-dozen turns Buddy Buck let his bicycle come down again to the ground. He switched off.

"What did I tell ya!" he said proudly to the fat Indian, who was waiting for him outside. "That big cat's quiet as a pussy. I told you I'd soon have him ridin'."

He had taken good care to have Black Lightning pushed back into his cage before the proprietor saw him. The Indian would not have cared what means Buck used to tame the black leopard, but Buddy Buck wanted to show what a wonderful hand he was at training wild animals. Using drugs would not win him much credit.

"Buck, you're a marvel," the ringmaster told him. "That will be a big hit for this evening. The Black Thunderbolt and his Black Leopard! I'll have some new posters made out."

"Sure thing, Boss. My turn'll knock the crowd cold," Buddy Buck assured him.

That evening the Negro gave the leopard some more meat with white powder on it. Black Lightning was still feeling sleepy after the dose of drug he had had at midday. He dragged the meat into the back of his cage but he was not hungry. It got covered over with straw.

When the time came for the show the gallery surrounding the Wall of Death was packed with people. The news had soon got about, how Buddy Buck, the Black Thunderbolt, had tamed a black leopard straight out of the jungle and was going to carry it on his death-defying ride. The audience waited impatiently as Buddy Buck did his usual tricks riding the Wall: taking his hands off the handlebars and snatching a handkerchief in his teeth from the fingers of a daring lady who dangled it over the edge. At last the big moment arrived. Black Lightning was trundled in on the trolley. A gasp of excitement sounded as the splendid black beast was urged out and seated on Buddy Buck's pillion.

Black Lightning still felt rather dazed, but his brain was clearing. He opened his mouth in a yawn which turned into a snarl as the engine started off with its deafening clatter.

"Look out, Buck," somebody shouted, but the Negro grinned vaingloriously, showing his fine, shining teeth as he glanced back at the fierce head so close behind his own.

"We're okay, ain't we, chum?" he shouted and roared away up the Wall.

For the first two circuits Black Lightning held on to his place, hardly realizing what was happening. He saw the flares flashing above in a giddy, horrible circle. He saw the brown excited faces staring down over the top, blurring into an unbroken ring as Buddy Buck swooped round and round. Was he dreaming? The noise, the machine's bangs and rattles, the lights, made him think of that frantic, mad rush through the forest with the guns and the torches all around him. His claws tightened instinctively as he grew tense to spring off in flight.

"Hi, steady there!" Buddy Buck shouted as he felt those claws gripping his shoulders and the weight of the rising leopard pressing upon him. He stared wildly down, his eyes rolling. The cylinder's bottom was empty, as it always was during his ride. He would have to descend. The great cat was upsetting his balance, making the machine wobble dangerously. He was throttling down, preparing to return to earth, when Black Lightning suddenly sprang. The downward force of his leap sent the bicycle and its rider crashing to the Wall's bottom, but Black Lightning soared through the air. His hooked claws caught the edge of the top. A horrified scream rose from the crowd of spectators, who fled in a panic, bolting and jumping like monkeys down from the gallery. But Black Lightning's hind feet had slipped on the smooth, curving surface. His grip failed, and he dropped with a thump inside the enclosure.

They had hauled Buddy Buck out. He was tough and he was not much hurt, though he had a slash on his neck from the leopard's claws. He staggered up, rueful and shocked, as the proprietor hurried up from the big circus tent.

"What goes on? What goes on, Buck, man?" he shouted excitedly. He had seen the panicking crowd jumping down from the gallery.

"Boss, I don' rightly know," Buddy told him, rubbing his shoulder. "That big cat went crazy or somethin'. Thought I had him gentled up. He's in there right now." He pointed at the Wall of Death.

"In there, loose?" The Indian's voice squeaked hysterically.

"We must catch him at once. Supposing he leaps in among us!"

The ringmaster started to shout. Men ran to him with yells of alarm. The animal tamer was called. He brought his chair and his whip while the others armed themselves with poles and hay forks. Someone glanced in through the Wall's door, but slammed it hastily, for Black Lightning's blood was up and he charged with a fierce cough of anger. Nobody dared to go in, though a few bold spirits who climbed to the deserted gallery shouted all sorts of directions. The circus proprietor flew into a terrible frenzy. He wanted the police and the fire brigade summoned immediately. He yelled for a gun, for hoses, for pieces of meat. He gave orders that everyone was to keep clear of the enclosure, inside which they could hear Black Lightning raging. They must leave him there for the night, the proprietor said. In the morning, if they could not catch the leopard they would have to shoot him. He was very loath to do this. He had paid a hundred rupees for the animal.

In the end the animal trainer came to the rescue. He was used to dealing with lions and tigers and, although he had no intention of facing the leopard, knew ways of subduing wild beasts. At his suggestion they threw Black Lightning a large juicy morsel of meat. While he was devouring it they dropped a net over him. When he was fairly entangled they dragged him back into his cage. After that he was left to himself in the menagerie. Buddy Buck had no more to do with him.

But although Buddy Buck looked a trifle shamefaced at the failure of his daring act, the proprietor was not displeased. The event caused quite a sensation and brought him a lot of publicity, which he loved dearly. All the time they stayed in Colombo hundreds of visitors flocked to see the black leopard that had upset the daredevil rider and frightened so many people.

11. Escape

Three weeks later the circus moved on. Before leaving for India it went to Kandy in the mountains, where thousands of pilgrims came at this time of the year to take part in the great Buddhist festival. At the time of full moon the Buddhists' most holy relic, the tooth of the Buddha, was carried through Kandy's streets in a splendid procession.

The big tent and the Wall of Death were put up in a field toward the edge of the town, close to the jail. Half the night the air shook with the roar from the motor-bicycle's engine and the yells from the innocent villagers amusing themselves on the primitive roundabouts and the Great Wheel, which were part of the fair. Half the night long, people came to the menagerie and stared at the wretched animals, rattling sticks on the bars of the black leopard's cage to make him open his mouth.

Black Lightning had grown very thin. His coat had become rough and dull, with rubbed sores and bare patches. He slept badly and ate very little of the poor food he was given. He was ready to die, for existence held nothing he loved, and his soul was too large and too free for him to be able to live out his life in a cage in a dirty tent's corner.

A boy bent to stare through the bars. When he saw the black leopard he started, looking up at the Buddhist monk whom he led through the throng.

"This is a black leopard like the one we saw caught with the elephants. Perhaps it is the same one."

"Perhaps it is, child," the old man said, shuffling on. He was weary after the excitement of walking in the procession and attending at the Great Temple. Only through kindness of heart had he brought the small boy to the fair, for his bones and his feet were tired out.

"Poor beast," the boy said, lingering. "He was happier far in his forest."

"It is his fate," the monk answered. "Like us, he must bear his existence, good or ill as his past lives deserve."

"Can no one help him?" asked the boy.

The old monk was walking away, his mind half on some other matter. "Ay, child, we may all help each other. That is our duty," he mumbled. "Do I not help thee, and thou me?"

The boy followed him out, but his eyes went back to Black Lightning, famished and sick. He had wanted to ride on the roundabout, to let off fireworks, but now he felt burdened by pity for the poor captive. How could he help him? he wondered.

That night, when at last quietness came and the flares of the fairground gave place to the twinkling of the fireflies at play, Black Lightning stretched out in his cage. His yellow eyes were half closed but he did not sleep. He was living again the old days, the swift sweeps through the jungle's green shadows, the walks between dew-heavy bushes with the hot sun waiting beyond. What had befallen him now? Why did he feel sad and weak? Why was he in this foul prison?

He heard a soft noise at his back. Something scratched at the tent's rotten canvas behind his cage. Then came a faint ripping sound. He heard two long, rusty creaks as the bolts of his cage were drawn back, first the top one, then the bottom. The cage door grated, and someone outside breathed quick words and then pattered away. Black Lightning smelled the fresh air, felt a faint draft playing about him.

Crampedly he contorted himself to turn around, facing at last front to back. He stretched out an exploring paw. The clean air blew strong in his face. The cage door creaked farther open as he pushed against it, then jammed against the tent's side. But that side had a long, narrow slit in it. Black Lightning wormed his way through. He was outside at last. He was free.

He wasted no time waiting there. Belly to earth, veiling the lamps of his eyes by keeping them low to the ground, he passed swiftly across the field and away to the shadowy trees.

The old monk awoke as the boy stole back to the veranda of the monastery where they both slept.

"Where have you been, my son?" he asked drowsily.

The boy had been trained to be truthful.

"I have been helping one who suffered great sorrow," he answered briefly but truthfully. In spite of his teacher's kindness to animals he was not quite certain what he would think of the leopard being let loose.

"That is well, child," the monk told him, nodded, and fell asleep once again.

Black Lightning kept away, as best as he could, from men and the dwellings of men. There were few about at this hour in the heart of the night, but some cartbulls winded him and snorted and stamped. One of the carters woke up and shouted at them. The leopard did not have to travel far before he came into a watercourse. He followed this up the hillside, where it widened out into a ravine filled with great tumbled rocks and thick bushes. Under their cover he trotted on through the darkness.

Toward dawn he heard a dog barking. *Yap-yap* it went in its foolish manner, yelping aimlessly at the sky, as long ago Black Lightning had heard another dog's barking while he followed his mother across the dry lake's bed. As she had stopped, so he now stopped, his round ears pricking. He had never yet tasted dog, but the sense had passed from his mother to him that dogs were good things to eat. He was hungry too. Already the fresh, clean air was swelling his lungs, making his blood race through him quickly and cleanly. Ah, how good a thing to be free!

He climbed out from the ravine and found himself at once in a forest of thick, dwarfish bushes. It meant nothing to him, but he had reached a tea plantation, such as cover the hills of Ceylon. The dog was barking outside a long, low, white building where the tea coolies lived and now slept. It was long since a leopard had been abroad in these fields, where the jungle had been destroyed to make room for the tea. Otherwise the dog might not have been yelping so boldly.

Something slipped out of the shadows silently. The dog never even whimpered. In a flash it was dead from a blow from Black Lightning's paw. The shadow went rustling away to feast in the ravine.

By sunrise he lay in a thicket far away from the town. The country surrounding him was half wild, half tame. He looked across a great valley with a broad yellow river winding through its middle and a waterfall at its far end where the hills soared up into clouds. In the valley were rice fields, patches of jungle, and villages in deep green woods of palms and enormous trees. Some of the valley was cleared into gardens of cocoa, cardamom, and tea. But much of it was still wild, and there seemed endless refuges for him should he have to take sudden flight.

He cleaned his fur and slept all through the length of that day—the first sound, health-giving sleep he had enjoyed for many long weeks. At evening he woke and yawned, staring over the valley. It was filled with the soft yellow glow of the evening sun. The rice fields twinkled with little runlets of water which ran down the terraced hillsides from one green field to the next. Up the valley a spot the size of a fly was moving slowly along the bank of the river. The black leopard's wonderful eyes distinguished it as a tame elephant, dragging a long piece of timber.

He got up and stretched. He was hungry again, but caution warned him that men were abroad in the valley. Dogs barked here and there in the villages, and from a white building a gong rang with deep, mellow chimes. As the sun set, hundreds of big dark fruit-bats flapped slowly across the red sky. Scores of them hung themselves in a tree over his head, squealing and bickering as they fed on its sweet-scented flowers.

He climbed up the trees, but the bats were too high and too cunning. They unhooked their leathery wings and flew noisily around him so that he retreated down to the tree's foot and set off to prowl in the valley. One of the barking dogs went suddenly quiet.

That night he discoverd a cave where he made himself comfortable. Its entrance was partly concealed by a snaking tangle of roots from a tree that grew out of the rocks. He slept well and kept hidden the next day, but as night came again he felt bolder and ventured abroad.

His acquaintance with men in the circus had made him no less wary of them, but now they were familiar creatures. He stalked silently near their villages, hearing their voices, smelling the smoke of their fires. For a few nights more he fed on their dogs and their chickens. The ease of their capture made him overbold.

12. The Great Black Devil

A drum throbbed softly among a small cluster of bushes. The drumming had gone on all day, sometimes louder, sometimes sinking down to a gentle, monotonous sob. When he first heard it Black Lightning's hair rose with suspicion. It reminded him of the tom-toms he had heard in the forest during the elephant hunt, and the bang-bang-bang of the drum in the circus tent. But as it continued hour after hour through the day his ears became used to its cadence, so that it ceased to alarm him. At nightfall he sauntered toward it. Something else had attracted him there, the bleat of a goat.

The black leopard did not know, but in the house he was approaching a man raved and rolled in a fever. The local *kapurala,* or witch doctor, had been called in and had diagnosed what was the matter. A devil, the Great Black Devil, had entered the man; so the *kapurala* had informed his relations and friends. There was only one cure for that. A devil-dancer must be summoned. He would frighten the devil away, and the man would be saved.

So all day long the drum had been thumped outside the sick man's hut. Offerings had been laid ready, and a goat had been bought and tied up ready for sacrifice. As evening fell

the drumming grew louder. The *kapurala* bade everyone sit in a circle. The fevered man was carried out on his bed and put down to await what would happen.

The drumming became even wilder. Then out of the trees there capered a fantastic and frightening shape. Bells jingled from its arms and legs, and on its head it wore a black mask, a mask of carved wood with huge teeth and white, glaring eyes. Its headdress was formed of a writhing collection of cobras, each with its hood widely spread, and out of its hideous jaws another snake wriggled. It pranced up and down in front of the invalid's bed; and each time it uttered its dreadful blood-curdling groan the sick man echoed its cry.

Whatever the human onlookers thought of this weird-looking apparition, there was one, unseen in its audience, who held it in no sort of awe. Black Lightning had come on the scene some time after the devil dancer had started his antics. Otherwise the flash of lightning (supplied by the *kapurala,* who had thrown powdered resin into the flame of a torch) which announced the dancer's arrival might have sent him bounding away. As it was, he saw only a group of brown men and women with another, obviously a human despite his odd dress and behavior, leaping about in their center.

The black leopard's eyes fixed on the goat. That was what he was after. That would give him a really square meal. The creature was tied to one side away from the drums and the torches, waiting its turn in the ceremony. Black Lightning crouched low in a dark mass of cardamom plants, waiting his turn too. His freedom had given him an enormous appetite, which dogs and chickens had subdued for only short periods.

The devil-dancer uttered a fiendish howl which would have set Black Lightning flying in the old days. But he had become used to noise and the yelling of men. The sick man answered the howl with one last dismal groan and sank back on to his bed. The devil-dancer stopped dancing. The drum stopped too. The *kapurala* had risen to say that the devil had now left the man when a great black shadow bounded past him, snatched up the goat, and disappeared into the darkness.

There were shrieks of surprise and fear from the terrified villagers. They believed that the devil really had come from the man and gone off, taking their offering. The *kapurala* turned pale, so far as his dark skin would let him, but he was quick-witted. He had to be in his job. Hastily he explained that there was no cause for alarm. He had everything under control. The Great Black Devil had gone. Everybody grew calmer at this, and they praised his skill when they saw that the sick man had at last broken into a sweat and was sleeping peacefully.

But although their fame was increased by Black Lightning's surprise visit, the *kapurala* and his friend the devil-dancer were both very annoyed about the disappearance of their goat. That goat, after having been offered up to the devil, was to have been part of their fee. It was not at all right for the devil to take it away.

In his spare time the *kapurala* was a hunter. Next morning he set off early with two of his friends, his gun, and a couple of dogs. It was not hard to trace where the devil had gone with his prey. They found its remains in a thicket, and the dogs followed Black Lightning's trail to the mouth of his cave.

After some discussion they decided to smoke out the leopard. They lit a fire, pushing it in and piling on heaps of leaves and damp grass till it sent out great billows of smoke. Much of this blew back at them, making them cough and their eyes weep, but a good deal rose into the cave and woke up Black Lightning, who was sleeping well after his meal.

He sneezed and sat up on the ledge where he had his bed. The cave was beginning to fill with the white, choking fumes. He looked up. Some way over his head was a small opening in the rock, where the tree's roots had prised it apart. He scrambled up to this hole and thrust his head into fresh air. The three men and the dogs were standing some twelve feet below. Black Lightning poised himself half in, half out of the rock, then suddenly sailed right over their heads to the ground. The *kapurala* shouted and fired his gun, but his eyes were so sore with the smoke that he could not see clearly.

"I believe after all it was not a leopard," he told his friends seriously, making the best of a bad job. "It looked very much like a devil."

His friends quite agreed. One of them was the devil-dancer.

But Black Lightning was traveling now. He hurried along for some miles, dodging among the rice fields, till he found a safe spot to hide in. Until night fell he rested hidden, then trotted on. Next day he lay in a wood high up in the mountains, having followed the wide yellow river till it became narrow, tumbling down steep, rocky gorges. More tea fields surrounded him now, stretching mile after mile, but here they were broken by islands and peninsulas from the jungle, which clothed all the ridges above. Should danger approach, Black Lightning had a screened escape, leading straight up to the forest.

At evening he was disturbed by the sound of a horn, which blew a long-drawn, wavering note that echoed through the mountains. But this was no summons to hunters. It was only the signal to tell the coolies to stop work.

In the twilight he climbed to the forest. This forest was different from any that he had known before. It was thicker, more tangled by far than the jungle down on the plains. It was all tilted steeply too, interrupted by ravines and streams. Wide, steep faces of rocks, cliffs and soaring peaks, broke its green mass. Its floor was a thicket of creepers, thorns and bamboos, nettles and succulent shrubs. Tree ferns with brown hairy stems rose high from its black moist soil, and the close-packed trees were covered with long skeins of hanging gray moss. No drought ever parched green things here. This was the tropical rain forest, whence the water which fell from the skies descended by numberless torrents to feed the great rivers below.

At first Black Lightning found it exceedingly cold as he traveled along through this forest, not knowing where he was heading. It was chilly at night when the clammy mists drifted in and out of the trees, shutting down whole sections of forest in their damp, blinding fog. Their dew beaded on his black coat, making him sodden and shivering. The rocks too were icy cold, and all day long dew or rain dripped from the dark roof of trees, so that he thought longingly of the hot sunny rocks in the plains. But he found dry warm earth-caves to sleep in, homes of his old friends the porcupines. He found game trails to follow, green tunnels through the vegetation. And he found something else: a broad trail down the spine of the ridges, winding around peaks and along the edge of precipices—a road trampled out long ago by the marching of elephant herds.

There was plenty of game to be caught. Sambhur lived in this green wilderness of mountains and valleys; wild pigs too, and red deer, besides monkeys and jungle fowl. The leopard fed well and grew strong. The cold made his coat grow till it shone again, healthy and sleek, thicker and softer than ever it could have become in the hot plains. His muscles soon hardened into swift-actioned springs, and his yellow eyes shone, bright and daring. He had won back his old splendid health. He moved through the forest, its king. But he met none of his own kind. He began to feel lonely.

His way took him after some weeks to a place where the forest expanded. Here were spreading meadows of grass with the jungle in copses among them. Fast, rocky streams coursed through these fields, with plunging falls and still pools of icy cold water. This seemed the end of the forest, for when he explored farther on he came to a breath-taking drop where the mountains fell away sheer, thousands and thousands of feet, to the sunny plains spreading below. Those plains reached out mile after mile, broken only by little blue hills and the glitter of lakes, to where very far away he could see the blue sweep of the sea.

Here in that healthy, high country he dwelt for some time. Hardly ever did he see men, though once he lay stretched on a branch above a sun-dappled pool while a white man, a fisherman, fished for a half-hour or more, unconscious of those eyes watching him. But men were to come in due season. The planters had a hunt club with a fine pack of hounds. They chased the sambhur and wild boar, running them till they stood at bay, when a huntsman delivered the death stroke with his long knife.

13. The Pack

He heard them first one fine morning as he stood on a jutting rock, staring over the plains. The early sun turned all things golden. The bright bushes and the long grass glittered with dew, and the air seemed to sparkle and sing. Strong life and the joy of living moved in the mountains, and the brilliant gold and green jungle fowl everywhere crowed their approval.

But as Black Lightning stared at the plains he knew he must go to them soon. There lay his home, and it called him. Also, within him stirred a desire for a mate. Yes, very soon he would find his way down there, down from the hills.

He heard the faint baying of hounds, coming closer, drawing away, as the hunt raced through meadow and forest. He had never heard such a noise before but he did not like it. His face was a model of curious suspicion as he sat listening to that far clamor. He was often to hear it again on those joyous mornings between the monsoons when the carefree planters went hunting.

He was lying in his favorite basking place, the spur thrusting out from the top of that desperate cliff where the mountains fell straight to the lowlands. He had no feeling of height (why should he with his sure feet?) though below him there lay a great abyss, now filled with dawn's swirling mists. He rose, stretched, and stared down the cliff's edge. Trees and bushes grew out of odd cracks in that vertical sheerness; he could hear monkeys moving among them, calling and shaking their leaves. If monkeys had ways there, could he not use them too? Perhaps he could find a way down if he followed their roads.

He heard a sambhur bell sharply, then the baying of hounds on a scent. Their music swelled, but it seemed ugly music to him. He bounded away across a clear torrent which, a hundred yards on, leaped over the cliff in a white, rainbow-spangled fall. Up to a small rock peak set about with thick trees he ran, to crouch on a ledge, watching what would come of the hunt.

Soon he heard the crashing of branches. Jungle fowl whirred from a thicket, planing with curved wings like pheasants. Then out of the tangle on the farther side of the stream there trampled a fine sambhur stag. It shook its wild, shaggy mane and went galloping over the meadows, its heavy horns flat on its neck.

The hounds' voices came closer. Here they came now, a dozen or more, coats patterned white, black, and brown, noses to the ground. With them there raced two tall dogs like heavy-boned greyhounds, kangaroo hounds from Australia, whose duty it was to run down their prey by sheer speed, holding it till the rest of the pack could catch up and bay it. These great hounds did not follow by scent. Their pointed noses were not meant for laying to earth. They depended on their keen eyes and the pace of their legs.

The hunt swung away after the stag, but three hounds casting around picked up the scent of the leopard. They were young, inexperienced creatures or they would have left it alone. Perhaps they thought it was a cat. So it was, but a cat to which few dogs would care to give battle. Yelping excitedly, they left the right trail of the sambhur to follow Black Lightning's scent to the little rock peak.

Black Lightning had no wish to meet them. He neither feared them nor thought of them as his prey, for he did not feel hungry. But to get away he must return toward them, or else take a flying leap to the meadow below, straight into the view of the huntsmen who came running after the pack. He rose and sprang into the bushes from whence he had come. An unkind wind carried his scent to the three truant youngsters. They set up a tremendous outcry and rushed in to meet him.

He was still in an awkward position. The rock close behind him was steep. As he turned to claw his way up it the first hound arrived. Black Lightning snarled, then struck swiftly. The hound dropped, its neck fairly broken, but a second came in its place. Black Lightning struck it down too, then scrambled his way to the peak's top. He crouched silently, lashing his tail, as the third hound, bewildered and scared, ran back whimpering to join its masters.

The noise of the hunt faded away down the slopes. As yet the men did not know what had happened to two of their

hounds. Black Lightning had made up his mind that the coast
was clear when he heard the pack coming back. Its voices
grew louder and louder, frantic and exultant, as if close on
the heels of its quarry. He stood up to watch cautiously.

He heard splashing and the clatter of hoofs. Along the
stone bed of the stream he saw the sambhur returning, but
now its pace seemed slow and labored. Jets of steam blew
from its nostrils, its flanks heaved and were blackened with
sweat. It stopped knee-deep in a long pool below where
Black Lightning was waiting, standing under a small waterfall so that only its antlered head and its rough, dripping
neck could be seen.

The noise of the pack sounded near. Down the stream the
two tall dogs came tearing with short savage yelps and fierce
eyes. The stag waited till one sprang to seize him, then his
head ducked and swung up again, hurling the dog from its
horns. But the rest of the hounds were in sight on the banks
of the stream. The stag turned and splashed out of the water.
It plunged through the trees into the meadow, the hounds
at its heels in full cry. It seemed to have gathered new
strength from its desperate plight for it galloped strongly
now, heading straight for the great cliff's edge.

From his vantage point on the small peak the black leopard
saw a lovely, terrible sight. Scarcely pausing to muster its
powerful haunches for the effort, at full gallop the stag shot
out over the cliff in a glorious bound, its leap carrying it
high in the air, so that its body sailed in a wonderful curve
before the force of its jump was expended and it plunged

down, down into space. Two of the staghounds followed it into the abyss. The rest raged and yelped on the cliff's verge till the hunters arrived.

Black Lightning sprang down from his peak to hasten away to the nearest dense block of forest. He discovered a sun-warmed rock where he dozed for the rest of the day, thinking little more of the hounds or the men who ran with them. But, had he known it, the huntsmen were talking about him. They had discovered the bodies of their two young pedigreed hounds, newly imported from England, and their wood lore told them what had killed them. They swore vengeance against the leopard, promising the next time they came they would bring guns and make an end of him.

It was not long before they returned. That day the black leopard had fed well, before the sun rose. He was drinking at one of the streams before seeking some place to sleep when he heard the cry of their hounds. He was nowhere near the peak from which he had watched them before, but, as the hounds' baying came closer, he ran up a tree to be safe and to see where they were.

He saw them in full cry some distance away. The hunters were keeping close on the tails of their pack. They were frightened to let the hounds travel too far ahead lest the leopard should lie in ambush and destroy more of them. They scrambled through thickets and swamps on the trail of a big-tusked old boar, but today they all carried guns.

Soon he heard the wild clamor as the hounds bayed the

boar in the forest and the hunters went in to kill. He sprang down from the tree, starting away for the jungle on a high ridge. He was padding along easily when he heard the hounds baying again. He halted and turned his head back, staring through the deep gloom of the trees where the cicadas sang in their hundreds. Were those dog-voices coming any closer? Yes, he was sure that they were. His long body broke into a gallop.

The hunters knew what their pack followed. They had seen the leopard's pawprints and guessed that he sought to escape. But they had a reckless new Master, determined to avenge the two hounds the leopard had killed. Whooping and shouting to cheer their animals on, the men raced along on the trail. The pack was still fresh, and its blood as well as its masters' was roused by the death of the boar. It was eager to tackle this new and unusual quarry.

For two miles Black Lightning galloped, circling and dodging, but the hounds still kept on his track. He was getting blown now. His belly was heavy with the weight of his morning meal. A hunting horn sounded behind him as he speeded through the trees. Then the trees ended suddenly on the edge of the meadows. As he went bounding across them the hunting horn sounded again. Across the grass from the wood's edge where they had been held waiting the two tall dogs came racing after him. He was as fast or faster than they, but now he was sluggish and tiring. When he reached shelter in a small coppice he decided to climb up a tree.

The big dogs rushed past underneath him. They stopped within a few yards and started casting about, confused, for their powers of scent were not good and they had lost sight of their prey. Presently, yelping and barking, the rest of the pack caught up with them. They too overshot where the leopard crouched in a branch some twenty feet up, but one or two wily old veterans soon brought the other hounds back. The pack's leader, a scarred and grizzled bitch, whined as she picked up his scent. Resting her paws on the tree, she stared up it and loudly gave tongue.

The black leopard snarled down at her, his yellow eyes glaring defiance. She yelped and leaped with excitement, so that soon the whole pack had flocked around the base of his tree, making a hullabaloo. He could hear the men hastening toward them, shouting to one another. In a moment they would be there; he had no time to lose. Black Lightning decided for action and dropped without warning among the mad, shrieking dogs.

Right and left he struck out. One of the tall dogs went down as it snapped at his throat. The other seized him by the shoulder while the rest surged frenziedly around him. He was smothered by scrambling feet, red jaws in which savage teeth threatened. Steam, dust, and bunches of hair whirled up from the struggle as the leopard rolled onto his back, kicking and clawing like fury. The clamor and screams of the hounds made a hellish and deafening noise. Somehow he shook himself free and bounded away up the slope. A shot roared and a bullet went whining close by his head. He raced on, leaping a stream, to find himself heading the way the sambhur had gone.

He was making straight for the cliff's edge. He heard alarmed shouts from the hunters as they tried to call back their pack, close behind his long, curving tail. The hunting horn squealed and squealed in frantic appeal, and another shot whistled and smacked into a tree a few inches away. Black Lightning kept straight on, on to the verge of the precipice, then out of sight over its edge.

This time none of the excited hounds followed their quarry to destruction. Although they appeared so bold, they had pursued the leopard with far more caution than when they chased stag or boar. Even in full cry, those in front had shown some reluctance to be the first to come up with him. So now, when he disappeared over the rim where that abyss waited, they had time to be warned of their danger and space to pull up. They yelled and bayed on the cliff's top till their owners came, panting and swearing, to whip them away out of danger. The Master stood staring into that void. The gray stone reached down, empty and sheer.

"Well, that's the end of that devil," he said, more or less satisfied.

But he was wrong.

14. Return to the Plains

Down the side of the cliff Black Lightning had dropped ten feet. He had jumped, twisting to one side where a tree waited for him, leaning out over the emptiness from a foot-wide ledge of rock. It shook horribly as he struck it, but his four paws had barely touched down when he rebounded onto the shelf. This was covered with grass and small groups of rhododendron bushes. By the time the men came to stare down from the cliff's top he was tucked away snugly in a thick, glossy-leaved clump.

He waited until the last sound of dogs and hunters had faded away. Then he began to explore. It was hopeless to try to descend straight down the face of the precipice. Only a lizard could do that. Below where he stood peering, it appeared to overhang space. Through the low, drifting wisps of cloud he could see rivers shining like thin strips of silver. The jungle looked a dull green blur, the lakes little pools.

Somewhere to his right and below, the monkeys were chattering softly. He padded gently toward them, finding a long, deep crevice down which he was able to crawl. This ended in a rock slope, very steep and worn smooth by rain and wind. It was damp and slippery too, but he had to attempt to get past it. Carefully he crawled out on its surface.

Once his paws slipped. Instinctively his claws opened, but they could not help. Scratching long white lines in the stone, he began to slide steadily down, with nothing to help him, nothing to stop him from plunging into the void. Then the claws of one frantic, outstretched leg found a purchase, a tiny ridgelet of rock. It halted his terrible slither, and, resting precariously, he gathered his hindlegs under him for a great spring. A short distance off was a broken buttress of rock on which bushes and grasses were blowing. Risking all on the single chance of that desperate effort, he made a wild leap to reach it.

His claws hooked their points in a wind-twisted bush, tearing it from its insecure bed. But Black Lightning had used that slight foothold to fling himself up to safety. His prospects looked better now. He found himself on a steep slide, scarcely better than vertical, but studded with rough knobs of rock, rhododendron bushes, and tufts of lemon grass.

That descent took two days; during the night he crouched on a cold, exposed ledge with the monsoon winds buffeting around him. Once he found himself midway down, three thousand feet from the plains, three thousand feet from the summit, on a hanging island of rock with sheer space below. Again he had to take a most desperate risk, climbing down a swaying, loose festoon of creepers, which tore away under his claws and through which icy water was pouring from a small cataract. Soaked and frozen, he fell the last fifteen feet.

But he found himself on a broad ledge where he dried in the sun. Late in the evening he entered a cave and fed on a fat, sleepy bandicoot. Then he drank, cleaned himself, and slept.

After that it was easier going. He had mastered the cliff, and his way lay through wild, broken foothills, which soon gave way to the true jungle, the hot jungle he knew and loved. Instinct and memory led him on toward the sea, heading by long, winding trails to the old places he remembered, the ruined fort and the rock drinking pool. These lay many miles from the mountains, but some directing urge held his course always toward them, as if he were guided by compass. After weeks of wandering he came at last to the rock pool.

Two other travelers were making their way to the rock where that little pool lay. A monk and his small attendant stopped on their road to call on the Government Agent, the white man who kept law and order over that wild stretch of the island.

"So it seemed good to me to come hither to finish my days," the old monk was saying. He had known the Government Agent long years ago when he had held office in the Great Temple at Kandy, and the Government Agent had been an acting assistant undersecretary on probation at Government House. "I have read how the holy Abbot, the ancient and much revered founder of my monastery, dwelt long ago in a cave made for him in the jungle by his king's pleasure. I have heard that the cave still exists."

"Yes, Reverend One, it exists. That I know to be true. But for longer than men can remember no one has dwelt there. The wild beasts use it as their den."

The Government Agent was fond of exploring the jungle. He knew the cave very well.

"I would not willingly rob the poor beasts of their home," the old man said simply. "It may be none is dwelling there now. At least I may go and see."

The white man could not help smiling. He asked gently, "Who will look after you? It is lonely there. What will you eat?"

"My disciple and I will prepare the cave for my needs. Water is there I have heard. And once in a month villagers will bring the small food I require."

"But, Reverend One," the Government Agent warned him, "of late men have told of a leopard which feasts upon man's flesh."

"Beasts I do not fear," the monk answered. "What are they but souls like ourselves? Nay, I seek only to live out the rest of my days meditating among the green trees."

The white man got up from his seat. "Reverend One, then farewell and good fortune. In one month or two I will visit you in your rock dwelling."

As they walked down the hot, dusty road the boy said, "I will stay and look after you in that wild place."

"Nay, child, it is no place for you," the old man told him. "It is well for such as I am, with life nearly done, to live among simple things, with nothing to disturb his prayers. But you must go back to the monastery to learn and, afterward it may be, to teach."

They plodded on down the hot, dusty road on their way to the forest.

Black Lightning saw that two leopards had lately been to the rock. He decided to linger near it to see who these strangers might be. His senses told him that one of them had been a male, so he knew that they could not be his lost mother and sister. The sun was setting when he heard the soft rising and falling call of a leopard approaching. He crouched hidden, not far from the pool. Then he heard the faint snap of a twig as out of the bushes a long shadowy shape appeared and started to drink.

She turned with a quick, startled snarl when she found him beside her. She was a splendid young leopardess, sleek-coated, graceful and lovely. In her Black Lightning saw the mate he was seeking. He rubbed his chin on her neck, growling gently with a growl that was nearly a purr. At first she was shy and showed her teeth at his love-making. But soon they were playing together among the rocks under the moon.

Like cats on a roof, they were sitting close to each other on the rock's moonlit ridge, the place where the black leopard's father had stood looking down at the hunters. Suddenly Black Lightning stiffened. Another leopard was coming toward the pool.

The harsh sawing sound of its voice drew nearer and nearer, and out of the dark trees stalked a light-colored,

squat beast. Black Lightning saw that it lacked a good
half of its tail. It drank furtively at the waterhole, then
looked up and spied the two others outlined against the
bright sky. At once it sank down, belly flattened to earth,
snarling evilly. It had followed the track of the female. Once
or twice they had met in the jungle, where it had tried to
force its attentions upon her. But she would have nothing to
do with it. Now, to its fury, it saw another, a strange black-
coated newcomer, sitting with her on the rock.

Black Lightning growled his defiance, his ears flattened
back, his teeth menacing. The other crouched, lashing the
stump of its tail, then suddenly started to race up the slope
toward them. It moved fast, very close to the ground in a
hurrying scramble, its eyes fixed and flaming with hatred. It
sprang furiously at Black Lightning, who reared up to meet
its attack. The two became locked in a tangle of close-
gripping legs, ripping claws. Tight together they wrestled,
rolling down the rock's slope. Screeching and snarling, they
tore tufts of hair from each other as each tried to fix his sharp
claws in the other one's stomach. The leopardess sat placidly
watching them, her feminine vanity flattered by the fight
being fought for her sake.

Over and over they rolled till they cannoned against a
sharp rock. Like two rubber balls, black and white in the
moon's brilliant floodlight, they exploded apart and crouched
glaring, bawling their spite. Then they hurtled together
again. The forest and night birds echoed their ear-splitting
cries.

As they fought, claw to claw, tooth to tooth, the black leopard noticed a rank odor about his enemy. It was like something that he remembered from the menagerie. Tainted meat? No. Man smell? No. Yet like something foul formed from the two. It served to add to his hatred of his opponent. The stranger was agile and cunning, but it lacked the black leopard's lightning swiftness of movement.

It was lying under him now, its thick forearms tight around his neck while with ferocious strokes of its hind claws it sought to disembowel him. Black Lightning drew in his own legs as a guard for his stomach. Using his foe as a spring-board, he suddenly tore himself free and sprang to one side. As the other rolled up on its feet Black Lightning struck out with that blow which had broken the necks of the hounds. His stretched claws struck the other's face fairly, ripping across it. Leopard's faces are made for a fight. They are blunt, bone and muscle well molded, eyes guarded by socket and brow. But this stroke tore his enemy's soft and sensitive nose. It closed one of its eyes and all but clawed off an ear. The strange leopard uttered a squall and stumbled away. Black Lightning followed, but the other turned tail and ran. It disappeared into the black jungle.

Black Lightning returned to the female, who still sat demurely on the rock's top. He started licking his wounds, which were many and sore. Presently he found that she was licking them too. Together they went to the pool for the drink that he needed. Then he started away through the jungle, she by his side.

15. The Eater of Men

The weeks passed, and they hunted together through the gay forest. They were never far separated, he and his mate. The old monk heard them calling one to the other as he sat by the little cave which he and the boy had turned back into a hermit's cell. When they first discovered him there, the two leopards were badly startled. The leopardess snarled and went running back into the trees, but Black Lightning lay silent, watching. The old man sat, calm and sedate, his legs folded neatly beneath him, his wrinkled face bent. He did not pay any attention when the black leopard stole from his cover, although he knew the leopard was there.

As the jungle grew drier they came often to drink at the pool. Soon they learned to take no notice of the monk in his pale yellow robe, the color of the parching leaves. They knew that he meant them no harm, and they meant none to him. As for the monk, he felt no fear. He loved all the wild creatures about him, the bears that came snuffling and snorting, the shy spotted deer, and the birds which flocked there.

The Government Agent visited the monk as he had promised.

"Are you contented here, Reverend One?" he had asked.

"Very contented. I find all I hoped to find."

"And nothing disturbs your peace?"

"Nothing. Everything here is my friend."

The Government Agent left him, a little worried. He had heard more tales of the leopard which fed upon men, and he feared for the old man's safety. He was glad when he heard on his return from the jungle that a party of white men were shortly coming to hunt it.

The leopard Black Lightning had fought had come from the forest farther south of the drinking pool. It was a sullen, solitary beast, which bore hatred for men except in one horrid direction. It was fond of eating their flesh. This amiable habit it had picked up on the road to the Hindu temple, which ran through its hunting grounds. Pilgrims sometimes died on that road from disease or old age, and the leopard had learned as a cub to enjoy human meat. It hated all men because men had declared war against it. Once it had been caught in a trap from which it had escaped only by the strength of its well-muscled forepaws. It had managed to prise the jaws open, freeing its leg, but for long afterward it had limped, and half of its tail had stayed behind in the steel teeth.

It had followed the young leopardess beyond its own boundaries, seeking her for its mate. After Black Lightning thrashed it in battle, instead of returning to its own country, it lingered not far from the rock. It owed Black Lightning a grudge and still hoped to take his graceful, newly won mate. It took good care not to be seen near the drinking pool whenever Black Lightning came, yet it seldom went far away, biding its time for revenge. It saw the old monk arrive with his youthful attendant. It watched them make the cave fit for a hermit to live in. And afterward, when the boy had gone, leaving the old man on his own, it had crouched there watching the monk, thinking its own evil thoughts. Sometimes, sulky and spiteful, it followed the two other leopards on their walks, at a safe distance. So it was that it discovered the fort in which they had made their den.

Soon after they met, Black Lightning had taken his mate to the ruined fort. It was little changed since he had left it. The porcupines still made their home there, and the old den was tidy and dry. In due time in that den three leopard kittens were born, two dark fawn and one black like its father. The black leopard was happy and proud with his young, healthy family. He hunted and killed for his mate, while the cubs grew sturdy and strong, tumbling about in the little shadowy chamber as Black Lightning himself once had done. The old porcupines had discovered long since they need fear no harm from the leopards. When they met now in the passage they no longer curled up in defense. Instead, they waited, a placid look on their fat, black, long-whiskered faces, while their neighbors retreated, swearing, to use the other entrance. All went well in the old Portuguese fort by the tumbling sea.

The rains ceased early that season. When the cubs were

still far too tiny to follow their parents it became necessary
for the mother leopard to leave them while she went to drink
at the rock pool. One sultry night she and Black Lightning
had stayed out longer than usual, making their first hunt
together since the leopardess became a mother. They returned to the fort as the first pink clouds glowed in the sky.

Black Lightning entered it first from the old entrance in
the sand dunes, while his mate sat and stared at the sunrise
before settling down underground to her mother's duties. He
knew at once something was wrong, for a faint, foul odor
hung in the tunnel, an odor he recognized. Hair bristling, he
hurried along it, but something lay in his way. One of the
porcupines sprawled on its side, its black and white quills
lying flat, its head crushed and bleeding. Black Lightning
snarled and pushed past its body, hastening into the den.

Two cubs, the black male and one of the females, lay
crumpled and dead on the floor. Something had seized them
and savagely bitten their necks. The third cub was not to
be seen. With a moan of anguish his mate rushed in to his
side. She nosed the lifeless bodies with a cry that sounded
like a sob.

They found the third kitten mewing and stumbling along
the dark, musty passage, toward the sea end. As Black Lightning had done at its age, it had ventured exploring, and
that had been its salvation. With a little whimper of joy the
mother snatched it in her mouth and carried it to the den.

That smell which still hung in the tunnel had told the
black leopard the identity of the killer. His fur was still stiff

with his rage. His tail thumped against the den's wall with impatient fury. Leaving his mourning mate to carry the dead cubs' bodies away from their home, and to care for the one that survived, he cantered back into the jungle.

Leopards have not a good sense of smell compared with the other wild beasts that require it for hunting or warning. In the tunnel his enemy's odor had hung plain and strong, but outside in the open air he lost it at once. He saw its tracks leading away, but he soon lost them too. All day long he searched through the forest, listening for the belling of deer, the alarm cry of birds, or the watch call of monkeys, which would tell where the killer was prowling. But he heard no sound, saw no sign. Toward late afternoon he decided to make his way to the rock pool. Perhaps it would come there to drink. He approached from the rock's farther side, where the hermit's cave was.

The old man sat outside his cell. He had scattered a handful of rice, and around his bare feet pecked and fluttered a pair of little green doves. Black Lightning stole quietly up to the top of the rock. From here he could see both approaches to the drinking pool. He crouched down, waiting, screened by a low-hanging branch from the watchful monkeys and parrots that might give warning to his enemy.

He heard a soft drone from the monk, who was murmuring prayers. It was drowsy and peaceful under the warm evening sun, but Black Lightning was tense with anger. His yellow eyes stared at the pool, then swung around to the rock's other side. Suddenly his white teeth bared and his legs tensed and rippled for action.

A round, ugly head had thrust itself out of the bushes, at the foot of the rock below where the monk sat and prayed. Its eyes were fixed on the old man in a greedy and hideous gaze. Stealthily it sneaked out of the cover, creeping toward him.

The old monk had seen Black Lightning come but had given no sign. He knew the black leopard well now and thought of him as an old friend. He welcomed all creatures that came to drink from the pool, which he and the boy had made clean when he came to the jungle. Perhaps in his deep, loving knowledge he knew how the black leopard's path and his own had crossed twice in his lifetime already, that the leopard owed his glad freedom to his kindly words to the boy. But he had not seen that other beast, the eater of human flesh, which was silently crawling upward, screened from his eyes by the cave's lip. The doves suddenly fluttered away. The old man jumped as past him came bounding a fury, a shining black terror, mouth wide and roaring with rage. Past his cave it sped out of sight; and then from below there arose the sound of a furious battle.

The monk rose and peeped over the ledge. Underneath him two leopards were struggling, legs tightly gripping each other, madly clawing and squalling. They rolled out of sight into the trees, but he could hear their battle continue. One must have broken and fled, for he heard the fight cease and then start again farther away.

The big pale-colored leopard had never intended to fight with Black Lightning again. It had had its sneaking revenge on his helpless cubs, and had come to the pool for a drink before setting off to its own country, miles farther south. But its blood had been roused by the killing under the fort. It was hungry too, and had hunted all day in the jungle without any success. For once more the game was drifting away to the rivers, and its hunting was handicapped by the constant lookout it must keep to avoid the black leopard. At evening, bad-tempered and famished, it made for the rock hole, but the sight of the helpless old man revived its blood lust. It would feast on the flesh that it loved before it turned homeward.

When Black Lightning attacked, it broke free as soon as it could. It abandoned all thoughts of its prey or of quenching its thirst. It thought only of getting away, for it had not forgotten its last battle with the black leopard. At a headlong gallop it started away for the south, but Black Lightning remorselessly followed. This time he was determined to kill.

Twice it broke free again, but at last Black Lightning caught and held it. The forest rang loud with the din of their desperate combat, the yells as the man-eater died under Black Lightning's teeth. Far away the old monk listened to it and knew of its ending. In the twilight he heard the black leopard's hoarse panting and stole to the top of the rock.

"You have fought well, my brother," he murmured, peering down at the shadowy beast so thirstily lapping. But he did not know yet that Black Lightning had saved his old life.

16. The Kill

That dry season was very long and severe. Day after day the sun drove through the bright, blinding sky, making any green thing that was left wilt and bow down to earth. The trees turned black under its furnace. No birds sang through the endless, stifling hours. There was nothing to hear in the jungle but the cracking of brown, twisted seed-pods, the rattle and rasp of dead leaves. Only the mightiest trees and the gray, fat cactus bushes stood up, defying the sun.

All the game seemed to have vanished. The two leopards found it very hard to win food for themselves and the cub. Much of the country was wasted by fierce jungle fires, which destroyed or drove off the last living things that remained. The sky filled with dull, heavy smoke, which hung low and dense over the forest.

Once, while the three were hunting miles out in the jungle, a fire started somehow (who knows how they start? Some say a drop of dew, or a piece of glass left by a hunter, concentrates the sun's beams, setting the forest ablaze) and came crackling and speeding toward them, so that they had to run for their lives with the horns of a red, flickering crescent creeping ahead on each side. They raced to the reedy

lagoon whose brackish water, seeping in from the sea, never sank to a very low level. There they took refuge while the fire galloped on down the coast, leaving them behind.

No sweet water was left except in the few and far rock holes. The bears dug in the dry river beds, but the moisture they sought was scanty and deep underground. They were hard-working laborers, the bears, with their digging and climbing for honey, and their work made them hot and thirsty. Sometimes Black Lightning met one or two as, each night now, he led his small family to the shrunken pool. The old hermit still lived beside it, sharing its dwindling water with the wild beasts.

But most of the black leopard's hours were busy with hunting for prey. Despite all the hardships of life through that merciless drought, he and his mate were unwilling to leave their own ground and the old fort as, four years ago, his mother had left with her cubs. Although very often now they slept out in the jungle, they still thought of the fort as their home, of which they had grown fond. Besides, their cub seemed too young as yet to set out on that long, weary journey to the distant rivers. They knew that, if they could but hold out, the dry weather must break into rain. Then the game would return and life would be easy again.

So they stayed, and Black Lightning was driven to strange stratagems in his hunting. For hours he would crouch in the reeds on the edge of the nearby lagoon, waiting a chance to snatch wild fowl if they would come close enough. They did not oblige very often, and his long watch usually ended with the impatient leopard bounding through the warm, shallow water, while the birds cried and wheeled over his head. He would leap in the air and fall back with tremendous splashes, clawing at the flapping wings, but he seldom had any luck.

He and his mate and the cub would parade the edge of the sea for miles up and down the coast, seeking in pools and sea caves for crabs and shellfish, which made them most horribly thirsty when they had eaten them. Sometimes, at the worst, they were even forced to eat earth, staring first at the sun till to their dazzled eyes the earth seemed like raw, red meat. Perhaps fortunately, there were no villages within many miles of where they lived. Otherwise without doubt the leopards could not have resisted the temptation of raiding them for cattle and dogs. That would have called down man's vengeance; and so far they had done no harm to man, and man had left them in peace.

Once a month a boat landed near the fort. Two fishermen would jump out and haul it ashore. Then they would set off through the jungle, bearing small loads of provisions and little, long-handled axes to protect themselves against bears. They carried rice, vegetables, and fruits to the old hermit, who had made this arrangement before he took up his lonely quarters. The fishermen and their fellow villagers were glad to subscribe to the offering, and the men vied to take turns in carrying it to the cave. The old monk's fame had spread throughout that part of the country. He was looked on as extremely holy, and the villagers were sure that their fishing and crops were blessed and increased by the merit they earned by this deed. The two visiting fishermen and the monk were the only men the leopards had seen in their country.

Once, wandering far in forest he scarcely knew, Black Lightning found himself under another great dark mass of rocks, such as rose here and there throughout the jungle. He saw a smooth slope and a wide ledge, to which he climbed. At the back of the ledge gaped a long, narrow slit of a cave, from which came a damp sourish smell. The leopard suspected water. He thrust his head into the cavern. Something stirred and squelched down in the blackness.

He might have known better, but, with some hope of finding a prey, he entered the cave's gloomy mouth. There was something down there besides water or mud or whatever lay on the den's bottom. It might be a small deer he had cornered, or one of those gray iguanas. Two baleful, luminous eyes, set close together, swung up out of the blackness and hung in the air close to his face. He heard a dry rustle and scraping, and he caught sight of huge, scaly coils, writhing, unwinding. He would have escaped but those horrible eyes held his own. They were claiming his will, mesmerizing him.

With a half-frightened snarl his mate sprang past and struck at the thing. The horror hissed savagely, and a cold blunt nose like a hammer struck the leopardess in the chest, bowling her out through the opening. But Black Lightning was freed from the spell. Growling, he struck and felt his claws slither along something smooth and hard. He was fighting no warm flesh and blood but some uncanny horror. He sprang back into the sunlight as the rock snake, whose lair he had invaded, writhed and hissed again with thwarted rage, then coiled down into the coolness of its dank cavern.

Once he attacked a buffalo bull as it made a solitary pilgrimage through the forest. Except in most desperate straits, no leopard would think of pitting itself against such a dangerous monster. Yet Black Lightning could not resist it. His own hunger and that of his family drove him to risk the assault. He crouched on a branch overhanging the bed of a river and dropped suddenly on the shoulders of the huge brute as it ambled morosely along. His forelegs clawed its neck. His teeth sought a hold in its throat. But the great bull bellowed with rage and lumbered away. Lowering its wide, crescent horns, it broke into a gallop, rushing ponderously through the trees, so that in no time Black Lightning was swept from its back. He fell to the ground, bruised and shaken, while the bull trampled bellowing on.

One evening, some miles to the south of the hermit's rock, they heard a new noise in the forest. They stalked close, exploring inquisitively, and found they had come to a track that led off the old temple road. They heard the voices of men and the jingle of bells from cart oxen as they tore tufts from a pile of rice straw. Carters and villagers sat around a crackling fire. The leopards saw a tent too, with two white men sitting outside it, eating their supper. What were these intruders doing? They would like to have caught a fat bull, but those were far too well guarded. After prowling around for a while the leopards returned to sleep under some trees near the monk's cave.

They were far too hungry to sleep well. After a few hours they started hunting again, from midnight till long after dawn. But they found no game in the forest. They had not fed for two days now. The cub was fretful and weak. Black Lightning stared at the sky. He sensed rain in the air though not a cloud was in sight. But last night, and for many nights lately, the lightning had flashed without cease low down in the northeast. Thunder had rumbled too, and a lonely peacock had screamed from the top of a tree. All those signs told of coming rain. Perhaps the rains would break soon now, and all would be well.

The next night they met with good fortune. They were working the jungle together, he and his mate, prowling through the trees silently with a few hundred yards separating them. Their old tactics were useless now—the tactics of singing a loud song to startle the game, making it betray itself by its cry of alarm or by its blind dash away from one hunter into the clutch of another. The only way now was to travel as softly as they could among the noisy litter of tinder-dry twigs and leaves, hoping to chance on some lonely beast unawares.

But tonight they heard a stag belling. Black Lightning halted to listen. Yes, there was no mistaking that proud trumpet call, far away through the trees. Quickly and silently, like shadows, they raced through the forest, ears cocked, eyes piercing the darkness. Their feet struck the ground on soft pads, then rebounded, straightening out, doubling under their long, speeding bodies. Suddenly they crouched and crept. They had come to a wide slab of stone where the sambhur stag stood. Something had alarmed it already, for its head and its antlers were high, its ears pricked wide. It struck its forefoot on a rock, making a vibrating, whining sound, as if the whole earth was a-tremble.

The two leopards separated, crawling around the rock's margin in opposite ways; tail-tips jerking, eyes fixed on their quarry. As at a signal, they suddenly darted toward it, low to the ground. With a clatter of hoofs the stag bolted, nose high, antlers flat, as it raced through the black, swinging branches. Black Lightning sped up alongside it. With a leap at full gallop he sprang onto its shoulders, then slipped over, dragging and bumping, long teeth in the stag's shaggy throat. He wrestled, clutching its neck so that it staggered, over-balanced and fell, both leopards on it. Its neck was broken.

They began to eat ravenously, starting at the big sambhur's hindquarters. When they had finished their meal his mate went to call the cub from where they had left her, while Black Lightning guarded the kill.

17. The Decoy

They feasted again the next morning. Then Black Lightning dragged all that was left of the carcass along the ground and up into the branches of a strong, thorny tree. There it would be safe from the jackals and smaller vermin. After that they all went to drink and rest through the hot hours.

In the evening when the black leopard returned to the sambhur's remains he found they had vanished. He prowled about, hungry again and annoyed. Something had been here and interfered with his kill, though what it was he could not tell. There was little to hold the scent in the drought-withered jungle, yet he felt the strain of suspicion. There were traces of some business here, broken boughs and a mass of sticks in the fork of a nearby wild fig tree. He had not noticed that before. Yet he paid little heed to these signs, for how could he reason what danger they might foretell?

That night he paced angrily around, still in search of their kill, but he found no trace of it. All three were hungry again, so that in the end, giving up hope of the lost meat, they moved back toward the old fort where sometimes wild pigs might be found by the lagoon's banks. They discovered no game then or the next day, but at last the clouds had

gathered and filled the whole sky. Any day now it might
rain.

Black Lightning set off alone in the evening. He must find
some meat for his family, meat for himself. For some hours he
stalked through the jungle, returning once more to the place
where the sambhur had fallen. He was still a short distance
from it when he heard an odd bleating cry. That was no
jungle creature. That was a goat! He had come across goats
in his travels through the villages and tea estates. But what
was one doing here? He could not guess; but goats were
meat, excellent meat.

He crept cautiously through the trees. Yes, there was the
goat, standing out in a glade by itself, a few yards away from
that tree in which he had hung the dead sambhur. What was
it doing out here, so far away from its owners? Was it a trap?
He knew that goats were not wild things and lived only
where men tended them. He circled about it uncertainly, on
the alert, raising his hoarse hunting chant to back up his
courage. His call made the goat bleat more loudly and jump
frantically in circles. Why did it not run away? By now he
was aching with hunger. His mouth watered for that juicy
flesh. Not stopping to wonder or care as to why it was
tethered, he rushed in to seize it.

The goat was a brave little creature. The men who had
brought it had covered its head with a cloth while the
hunters climbed upon the platform built in the fig tree. As
far as it knew, it was left all alone in the forest, and this had
made it bleat plaintively, crying for help. Its crying had

summoned the leopard, as they had hoped it would. Its life was at stake, and it knew it. When it saw that fearsome black shape with its shining eyes it bleated loudly and lowered its little pointed horns. Black Lightning was so surprised that he paused for a moment.

A blinding beam flashed from the fig tree. In it Black Lightning stood dazzled and sharply outlined. Then the roar of a shot rang out in the echoing forest. The black leopard felt a terrific blow high on his shoulder. It knocked him clean off his feet, but he jumped up and stumbled away, growling and dodging the light, which chased here and there after him. He felt robbed of all sense by the shock. He could scarcely think, scarcely see. Onward and onward he dragged himself, panting and feeble, a trail of dark blood following him. He was worn out and terribly thirsty, and the wound was a great aching misery. At long last, led by instinct, he crawled painfully up the rock by the hermit's cave, then down to the little shrunken pool. He crept to it and gulped thirstily. Then he stretched flat on the stone, silent and motionless.

At first light the old monk rose and prayed. He lifted his face to the skies. The clouds were packed there in thick masses.

"Rain soon," he murmured, "and bring fresh life back to this forest."

His staff in his hand, he climbed slowly to the rock's top, on his way to the pool to fetch water. He saw the leopard's sprawling body. The blood trail ran over the rock, passing his cell.

"What is this, brother?" he whispered. "Who has done this evil to you?"

He was starting to shuffle down to Black Lightning when he heard branches rattle as someone pushed through them on the far side of the pool. Two brown men came into sight, their faces bent to the blood trail the black leopard had left. One of them looked up. He opened his eyes and his mouth in surprise when he saw the monk standing above them on the rock's ridge. He nudged his companion. Both of them stopped. They had not known the trail they followed was leading them to the monk's cave.

The old man pointed a lean, shaking finger at them. "What do you seek here?" he asked.

They held up joined reverent hands, for they recognized him as the hermit of whom they had heard. They were simple villagers, hired by the white men as trackers, but in their own primitive fashion they followed the Buddha's teaching and showed great respect to his monks.

"Holy One, we came not to disturb you," they stammered. "We do but hunt a wild beast."

"What manner of beast?" the monk asked, and the men trembled at his expression. He looked very angry.

"Holy One, a vile eater of men's flesh. The white sirs have shot it and offer reward for its finding."

"Describe this beast," ordered the monk. He was sure Black Lightning was no eater of human flesh.

"Reverend One," one man began, "it is pale and squat-shaped, with a tail which has lost half its length—"

Here the other interrupted to say, "True, brother, such is the man-eater. Yet, the white sirs say that the beast they fired on seemed black."

"Oh, wicked men," cried the old monk, and he beat on the rock in his rage, "how dare you follow it here, where the very stones by my cave bid you show kindness to all living things?" He pointed to the old inscription which he and the boy had made clear again. The villagers fell on their knees. In their ignorance they feared lest he might put a curse on them. "Go back to your white men," the monk said, "and tell them their man-eater's bones and skin lie in the forest, a few miles south of this place. Hunt for them well and you will find them."

"But, Holy One, the blood trail—"

"Speak no more to me of blood," the monk told them fiercely. "Turn back and obey me now, or—"

They bowed their heads to the ground. They swore they would do as he bid them. Nothing, neither reward nor threat, would make them bring the white men near his rock. Then they got up from their knees and ran into the jungle.

The old monk descended the rock on its other side. He did not go close to Black Lightning because, though he feared nothing and loved all creatures, he certainly was not a fool. A wild leopard is only safe for a human being to touch when it is really and truly dead. And Black Lightning was not dead. The monk could see that.

He stared at the splendid black body with the cruel wound in its shoulder.

"So you fought with the killer of men as he crouched close to my cave?" he murmured softly. "Perhaps he desired my old flesh, tough though it is. For that service I thank you, my brother. Well, I do not think *you* will die, for that wound is too high to be mortal."

And just then the first heavy raindrops came tumbling down from the sky. Plop, plop, they fell into the pool. Some parrots went screaming wildly above his head as the thunder crashed over the forest. Black Lightning opened his long yellow slits of eyes and dragged himself onto his feet for another deep drink from the pool.

18. Sanctuary

The forest was filled with a green mist of leaves once again, cheerful with birds' bright feathers and their gay calls. Where the fires had burned, fresh grass grew. Everywhere the wild animals roved, the buffaloes in their gray herds, the elephants caked with red mud, the rough sambhur and sleek spotted deer. The bears rushed about like noisy, mischievous boys, squabbling and making love with scuffles and horrible bawlings. The two leopards and their well-grown cub lived in their old den in the fort. It was dry and comfortable there. They often came to drink at the hermit's rock pool.

Black Lightning's wound had healed well. It had made him limp badly at first, but now he was as agile and fast as ever he had been. He was proud and splendid to see, the king of all this jungle country.

Though the monk had prayed for the wet weather, it made his old joints very stiff. With his staff aiding him, he tottered up to the rock's top to bask in the sun. Presently, like a tortoise's, his head turned on his thin, wrinkled neck. He thought he had heard footsteps coming. Yes, someone was walking toward him; but not till he came very close did the monk recognize his old friend the Government Agent. They greeted each other affectionately.

"All goes well, Reverend One?" asked the white man.

"Excellently, my friend. And you?"

"I come here on duty. The government has ordered that a game sanctuary be established. I am to define its boundaries."

"That is well." The monk pondered a moment. "Could it be that my rock might be included within this sanctuary?"

The other unfolded a map. Before his friend spoke he had had such a plan in his mind. "I had thought to forbid any hunting in a circle sixty miles wide, with your rock as its center," he told the old man, who put on some spectacles pulled from a case in his robe, to study the map that he offered. Except for a portion of sea on the side of the fort, that circle held in it a noble stretch of wild country.

"Good." The monk handed it back with a nod of approval. "It is right that there should be someplace where wild creatures may live without interference from men. By this action you will win merit."

The Government Agent laughed. "The government will acquire merit. I did but provide the thought. By the way, you have increased *your* fame in the villages lately."

"How is that then, my friend?"

"You told some men where to look for a certain man-eater. How on earth did you know he was dead, and where they would find his remains, bob-tail and all?"

The old man chuckled. "I have a friend here who told me

where they might be found. If you wait you will probably see him."

Puzzled, the white man sat down beside the hermit. Evening was drawing on, and, as they sat quietly, the wonderful pageant of animals came to drink. There were pigeons and peafowl, and the smaller creatures, porcupines, wild cat, and mongoose. Deer came, and bears, and the old lonely elephant bull. Then from the trees Black Lightning walked out with his family.

"What a magnificent beast," the Government Agent exclaimed. "I'd heard a black leopard had been around here, but *I've* never seen one before."

"That is my friend," the monk said, and he went on to tell how the black leopard had fought the man-eater under his cave, and how, far away, he had heard the end of that battle.

"Well, by Jove," said the Government Agent, "he deserves a long life after saving yours from that horrible bob-tailed brute. And he'll get one too, providing he keeps in the sanctuary. I'll issue an order that he's under special protection."

Black Lightning was drinking contentedly down at the pool while his mate and her daughter sat grooming each other's sleek speckled coats. Presently the three stood and stared up the slope at the two men on top of the rock. Then, unhurriedly, they turned and strolled away into their jungle.